TIME LOCK 3:
THE MILLENNIUM PARADOX

TIME LOCK 3: THE MILLENNIUM PARADOX

HOWARD BERK
AND
PETER BERK

IE Snaps
by
IngramElliott

**The *TimeLock* series by
Howard Berk and Peter Berk**

A sci-fi-tinged action-adventure with heart and humor, the *TimeLock* series is set in the crime-ridden near future where a bold new technology transforms the justice system and challenges America's moral compass. Only one problem—what happens if you're innocent?

TimeLock

When everyman Morgan Eberly is arrested for a murder he didn't commit, he's subjected to an experimental new technology that instantly ages prisoners the number of years of their sentence. Now forty-three and on the run, can Morgan and rogue FBI agent Janine Price unlock the truth about TimeLock before it's too late to turn back?

TimeLock 2: The Kyoto Conspiracy

Two years after the events of *TimeLock*, Morgan Eberly and Janine Price are forced to journey from DC to Japan to Siberia to prevent the development of a new weaponized form of TimeLock authorized by the unhinged and deadly new President of the United States.

TimeLock 3: The Millennium Paradox

A radical prison experiment based on TimeLock's genetic acceleration technology gives a convicted killer superhuman powers that threaten a small Alaskan town and quite possibly the whole world.

Coming Soon

TimeLock 4
The exciting next chapter of the *TimeLock* series.

Dedication

To two people whose love, humor, kindness, and support have made them both true heroes in the story of my life: my beloved cousin (and fellow writer) Julie Fenster and best friend since we—and the world—were young, Ken Reiter.

ACKNOWLEDGMENTS

Four books in, I'm more grateful than ever to the brilliant team at IngramElliott for their warmth, inspiration, and creativity. Of all the words I've written over the years, the ones in the query letter I sent to them about my first novel, *TimeLock*, may be the most professionally consequential and rewarding of them all. Thank you more than I can ever say and I look forward to being a part of the IngramElliott family for many years to come. Also, a special thank-you to the late producer Phil Rogers, who worked closely with me and my dad on the story of the original screenplay on which *TimeLock 3* is based.

PROLOGUE

FIVE YEARS AFTER THE EVENTS OF *TIMELOCK 2: THE KYOTO CONSPIRACY*

Inside the SUV, Tom shut off the engine and was about to get out. But the door wouldn't open. He pulled up the door lock lever, but it went right down again. He tried it once more, but the same thing happened. Then Tom heard the back door slam shut and the vehicle suddenly began moving. He tried applying the brakes, but to no avail.

Tom turned around. The figure in the back seat was smiling. And Tom could tell right away that he had changed since their last encounter: the silvery sheen of the hair was more pronounced, the skin had taken on a richer metallic gloss, and the eyes were farther apart by several millimeters.

"Nice day for a joyride," he said.

The SUV suddenly shot ahead at head-snapping speed. Tom's instinct was to fight the wheel and stomp the brakes, but it was useless. Then he looked on in shock as the car raced out onto a long pier.

"You'll kill us both!" Tom yelled, but his passenger just continued to smile. The SUV then crashed through the barrier at the end of the pier and dove toward the water. But instead of splashing in, it remained just above the surface, skimming along rapidly like a hovercraft.

In the back seat, the figure seemed to be having the time of his life. Realizing it was pointless for him to hold the steering wheel, Tom let it go and whirled around.

"What are you?"

"Don't ask too many questions. You may get in over your head."

Now Tom looked forward again. And for all his cool, his mouth parted as the SUV slowly slid beneath the waters of the bay and angled down, then leveled out and soared forward.

CHAPTER ONE

AUGUST 2039
KYOTO, JAPAN

It was another sleepless night after another momentous day in the life of Yoshi Ito. And in just three decades on this Earth, he had already lived through more than a few momentous events.

This night, he again promised himself to finally cast aside the guilt that had tormented him these last two months. It wasn't his fault—as he had been told so many times. And at long last, he was starting to believe it.

But even though the guilt was finally receding, nothing could keep the memories from swirling in his mind. Memories of science gone astray—something Yoshi was well acquainted with as the result of what his sister, brother-in-law, closest friends, and he had experienced firsthand five years ago both in the United States and in his native Japan.

Though five long years had passed, it all sometimes seemed like yesterday to Yoshi. Beginning with the wildly controversial program called TimeLock that his brother-in-law—the famed geneticist Dr. Louis Garrett—was forced to develop.

Through the application of a radical new genetic acceleration technology, TimeLock instantly aged inmates the number of years of their sentence as an alternative to serving conventional prison time. A conscientious man whose life goal was to help ward off the effects of aging, Dr. Garrett wanted nothing to do with the program, considering it immoral, unethical, and an affront to both God and science.

Unfortunately, however, his boss—a sociopath named Patrick Loder, CEO of TimeLock's parent company Genescence—threatened Dr. Garrett and his wife, Yoshi's beloved older sister Kiyoko. Fearing for Kiyoko's life, the doctor had no choice but to go along with Loder's plans for TimeLock—plans that were heartily endorsed by no less than the future President of the United States, Myra Winters.

And then the first of several tragic events came to pass. Unwilling to test the TimeLock process on anyone but himself, Dr. Garrett was accidentally aged thirty years in a matter of moments. And in part to cover up that fact, Loder insisted that the thirty-five-year-old Louis Garrett be replaced by the sixty-five-year-old "Dr. Lionel Garvey."

Later, when the TimeLock process was seemingly perfected, Myra Winters coerced the reluctant President of the United States, William Bartlett, to immediately authorize the program as a means of curtailing the country's astronomically high crime rates. And, for a time, even skeptics like Yoshi had to admit that the notion of "three strikes and you're old . . . very old" did, in fact, prompt countless potential criminals in America to choose working and saving over breaking and entering.

Regrettably, though, it turned out that TimeLock was as flawed technologically as it was morally since Loder had rushed his billion-dollar program to completion, despite Dr. Garrett's vociferous objections. And the world may never have learned of those flaws but for one brave man—an innocent inmate named Morgan Eberly, who had been aged from twenty-three to forty-three before managing to escape prison, team up with FBI agent Janine Price, expose the truth about Loder and Genescence, and ultimately bring both crashing to the ground.

Two years later when TimeLock seemed relegated to the past, however, newly elected President Myra Winters authorized the kidnapping of both Dr. Garrett and Kiyoko from their home in Kyoto, Japan. The goal this time wasn't to force Louis to reconstitute the old TimeLock prisoner program, but to modify the process in order to genetically impair enemy combatants on the battlefield. In her twisted mind, it was later revealed, secretly violating international laws against biological weapons would be an acceptable course of action if TimeLock's powerful genetic alteration formulation would be able to instantly physically and mentally weaken enemy soldiers during times of combat.

This is where Yoshi came in—joining Morgan and Janine (by then an unlikely but devoted couple), along with several brave and honorable friends of Yoshi's in Japan, to find and rescue Dr. Garrett and Kiyoko. As it turned out, they had been captured by two Myra Winters loyalists—a military advisor named Sloane Whalen and Brigadier General Carter Prescott. While Sloane Whalen met her demise in Japan, Prescott not only got away but took with him the last remaining supply of kalopheen—the rare mineral that made the genetic alteration process behind TimeLock possible.

Back in America a short time later, on the eve of Morgan and Janine's wedding, Dr. Garrett was able to give his friend the most unexpected wedding gift imaginable—he had found a way to reverse the TimeLock process. But there was an enormous catch. Prescott had set up shop this time in Siberia, so once again Morgan and Janine were called to duty to stop the president's crazed program before it could even get started and to retrieve the stockpile of kalopheen they needed to reverse the effects of TimeLock. At great personal risk, they soon took part in a US Special Forces raid on Prescott's new facility in Russia—a mission that wound up ending both the program and the brigadier general himself.

But one target managed to elude their grasp—a Russian geneticist named Sergei Baranov who had joined forces with Prescott and was last seen falling into a raging river in Siberia. Little did anyone know at the time that not only had he survived the fall, but that he would prove to be an even greater threat to humanity five years later.

Returning to the States from Russia, Morgan was ready for his next life-changing adventure—finding out if Dr. Garrett could indeed give him back the twenty years he lost to TimeLock (and if the doctor could get back the thirty years he himself had sacrificed in the lead-up to the program).

As a jubilant Janine, Kiyoko, and Yoshi looked on, Morgan did in fact again become the twenty-five-year-old he would have been without undergoing the TimeLock process, and Louis Garrett was miraculously given back the thirty years he had lost as well. A happy ending for all concerned. Including for a young, newly orphaned teen named Mikhail whom Morgan had befriended in Siberia and brought back to America and who Morgan's mother soon adopted into the Eberly family.

A happy ending indeed. At least for a while.

A short time later, Yoshi took a new position in Washington, DC, under Dr. Emory Layton, the CEO of GenQuest Bio-Tech (formerly Genescence), who was carrying on research very similar to that being conducted by Dr. Garrett in Japan. Both men were chasing the same breakthrough—a way to advance human genetics to the point where people might fully recover sooner from life-threatening diseases associated with aging or even prevent their onslaught altogether.

After relocating to DC, Yoshi decided to enroll in an exhaustive molecular biology doctorate program and earned his degree eighteen months later. Coincidentally, around that same time, Dr. Layton's patience with both the crowds and the bureaucracy that permeated Washington had worn out. So he decided to relocate his entire nascent team at GenQuest Bio-Tech to a little fishing town outside of Juneau called Caribou Bay in his native Alaska. And since Yoshi was more interested in the work than in the address, he was among the dozen or so team members who enthusiastically agreed to the move.

One year ago, the year Yoshi turned thirty, everything seemed to fall into place for him once and for all. First, he loved his work and had only the deepest possible respect for his boss, Dr. Layton. At sixty-five, he projected a genial air of wisdom and dignity that reminded Yoshi of his brother-in-law, Louis. And second, GenQuest Bio-Tech was doing important, potentially even game-changing, work in the field of genetics and disease prevention.

What really made Caribou Bay come to life for Yoshi, though, wasn't the town's natural splendor or old-fashioned charm. It was a young woman named Katie Wayne, a local real estate agent who had recently relocated there from Los Angeles after breaking up with a longtime boyfriend.

In Yoshi's mind, the idea that an inherently shy, somewhat short, and slightly pudgy man like himself would ever attract a beautiful woman like Katie would be laughable to just about anybody. But as it turned out, Katie had been disappointed by a series of jocky, matinee idol types and was ready for someone kind, funny, and reliable. For reasons Yoshi never could quite comprehend, she found all of those qualities in him and more.

As Yoshi saw it, Katie was way out of his league, but then he realized she never once made him feel unworthy. When she chuckled at his jokes, he never felt they were pity laughs. When she expressed interest in his work, he never sensed she was just being polite. And when she kissed him, it never felt as if she were just doing him a favor.

Within weeks, Yoshi and Katie were not only a couple, they were in love. And after she accepted his marriage proposal, he went to the Bayside Inn to reserve a night in September for their wedding—coincidentally running into a local acquaintance named Tom Brooks who was there to plan for his own wedding ceremony and who was destined to play an integral part in what soon would happen in Caribou Bay.

Alas, a September wedding wasn't meant to be. Katie was diagnosed with stage four cervical cancer a few weeks later, and their world collapsed on top of them. With the likelihood of Katie not surviving until September, Yoshi suggested they marry right away, but Katie wanted to explore any and all treatment possibilities first.

And that's when Yoshi inadvertently condemned much of Caribou Bay to unimaginable destruction. While Dr. Layton wasn't an oncologist per se, his life's work was in disease prevention and mitigation. And so, Yoshi begged him to help Katie however he could. His only option, he said, would be a highly risky process—a new application of a cellular regeneration treatment Louis Garrett had explored prior to developing the TimeLock process which utilized the natural compound that made genetic alteration possible—kalopheen.

Dr. Layton repeatedly warned Yoshi and Katie that this new treatment would likely fail and could even prove fatal. But with a death sentence hanging over Katie's head anyway, she had nothing to lose by giving the treatment a try.

A week later, Dr. Layton began administering Katie's daily kalopheen doses. The results were moderately encouraging, but soon after, the whole endeavor hit a snag—Dr. Layton's supply of kalopheen would quickly be depleted. And then Yoshi had a brainstorm—what if he could take Katie back to Japan with him and let Louis continue what Dr. Layton had started since he still had some of the precious compound retrieved from Siberia?

Two days later, Yoshi and Katie were in Kyoto—where they remained to this day—never imagining that Dr. Layton would be encouraged enough by Katie's apparent remission to try a radical new experiment that would affect not only the future of the small town of Caribou Bay, but quite possibly portend the future of the human race itself.

CHAPTER TWO

Bright lights shone from several guard towers surrounding this recently constructed, state-of-the-art complex. Solid structures could be seen beyond a courtyard which was enclosed by imposing gray stone walls.

The complex was set in an isolated stretch of rugged coastline backed by towering snow-covered mountains. An area designated for employee housing was situated a quarter mile away from the prison grounds. A single road led into the complex.

An approaching storm flashed across the dawn sky with distant lightning and far-off rolls of thunder. Inside a new wing of the complex was a high-tech medical bay.

The lone figure inside the dimly lit, pristine white room rose and moved toward the door. Still several feet away from it, he concentrated intently, and the tumbler on the locking mechanism began to slowly turn.

The door swung open by itself, and the figure moved through it, then down a corridor to a stairwell. He continued up a flight of stairs, carefully avoiding a pair of guards, then made his way outside into the prison yard.

The interplay of lightning, thunder, and the occasional flash of beams from the guard towers created a distinctly surreal atmosphere. Shadows rearranged around the football-field-size courtyard, which was enclosed by forty-foot towering walls on all sides.

As the tower lights continued to sweep through their pattern, the figure began running faster, soon reaching an unfathomable speed and heading directly for one of the high walls straight ahead. He jumped and soared a full forty feet into the air before gracefully landing on top of the wall.

The figure then jumped off the other side and touched down on the rugged ground below that was surrounded by forest just beyond. Like the lightning that was blanketing the sky above, he sped through the forest and up toward the mountains ahead.

After a short distance, the figure reached the bank of a river, roaring its way toward the ocean below. The distance from his side of the river to the opposite side was at least 150 feet. He remained in place for a moment, then focused on the surging river just ahead.

Moments later, the water straight ahead began to lift midair. The water continued to flow downriver, but was now arcing in an upside-down U-shape, creating an archway to pass through. The river bottom directly under the archway was clearly visible as the passageway extended from this side of the riverbed all the way to the other side.

The figure moved through the newly formed passageway, briefly pausing to look up at the galloping river flowing only a foot above and then resuming its normal flow just off to his right. He smiled proudly at what he had done.

When he finally emerged on the other side, the figure turned back toward the flowing water—still suspended in midair. He focused, and the water came crashing down again. The river returned to normal as if its 650-year-old course had never been altered.

The figure continued running. He knew exactly where he was and exactly where he was going. The

quaint little town of Caribou Bay was about to welcome a new visitor.

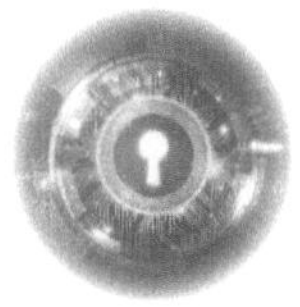

CHAPTER THREE

Even without losing their parents within a four-year stretch, Tom and Cooper Brooks were destined to have a rough childhood. Born and raised in the small Alaskan town of Talkeetna in the shadow of Mt. McKinley, theirs was a true frontier life, even with the modern amenities available to them growing up in the early twenty-first century.

Five years older than his brother, Tom was only thirteen when their mother, Annette, succumbed to lymphoma. Three years later, their father, Alex, a pilot with Alaska Airlines, was killed by a sudden lightning strike in his Beechcraft Bonanza when attempting to take off for Anchorage from Talkeetna's small local airport.

The boys were shipped off to Oregon to live with their paternal aunt, Beth. A humorless woman who had never married, she had frequently taken care of the two brothers after their mother's death and during their father's many work-related absences.

Around this time, it became clear to everyone who knew them that the Brooks boys were drifting further and further apart in terms of character, demeanor, and even looks (Tom being tall and well-built with light-brown hair, the five-foot-ten Cooper being thin and wiry with almost jet-black hair). Old enough to eventually pivot away from anger and sadness, at eighteen, Tom instead committed himself to honoring the memory of his parents. Indeed, he would do everything in his power to be as reliable and nurturing as they had been. And one day, he would be not only the best pilot in the state, but the best husband and father as well.

Cooper, however, went an entirely different direction than his "holier than thou" brother. The wounds of loss flared inside him unabated. Too young to channel his emotions in a positive way like Tom, Cooper instead turned inward. Life wasn't a gift—it was a challenge. Other people weren't a help, they were a hindrance. Never again would he invest his love or trust in anyone else because he knew one day they would inevitably be gone too.

By the time Cooper turned thirteen, he was out of control. School fights. Drinking. Smoking. Stealing. He not only knew he was a bad seed, he delighted in it. Unlike his saintly, boring, all-American hero brother, Cooper had a special identity. He was different. And because kids and even adults feared the rough-and-tumble teenager with the perpetual cold streak and unpredictable temper, he had the best thing of all. He had power.

When Cooper turned seventeen, his aunt—with Tom's complete support—shipped him off to a regional military school. Perhaps the school's strict standards of discipline would set Cooper straight after so many years of drifting and rebellion. Perhaps the now twenty-two-year-old Tom would finally get his little brother back.

Unfortunately, it wasn't meant to be. Within a week, Cooper escaped the school and was nowhere to be found. Despite endless searches by police, family, and friends, Cooper remained in hiding for almost a full year. By then, Tom had moved back to a picturesque small town in Alaska called Caribou Bay after graduating with a business management degree from the University of Oregon. But sitting behind a desk wasn't part of his grand plan. His plan was to combine his growing skills as a helicopter pilot with his newly learned entrepreneurial acumen and start his very own business. Two months and one nerve-wracking bank loan later, Brooks Helicopter Service (Tours & Instruction) was born.

With Alaska home to a huge number of military veterans yearning to fly a chopper and with a growing contingent of tourists anxious to see the state by air, Tom's business enjoyed almost immediate success. So much so that he was able to upgrade to a Bell 206 in only a year.

Life was good, but at the end of Tom's first year in business, his brother returned with a vengeance. Over time, it seemed Cooper had escalated from petty crimes to armed robbery. As Tom eventually learned, his brother had been lying low the past few months in a variety of small Northwestern towns, supporting himself with odd jobs and the occasional pool hustle. Low rent theft soon followed—mainly snatching purses and wallets—but eight months earlier, Cooper graduated to more challenging and lucrative jobs.

Prime among these was robbing convenience stores with his recently acquired Smith & Wesson. At first,

Cooper kept the gun unloaded, but eventually he realized having a loaded weapon gave him an added dose of power. And he liked that feeling. A lot.

What he didn't like was getting caught. But his luck ran out one day while holding up a gas station mini-mart near Seattle just when a couple of off-duty cops happened to be picking up some snacks. Cooper was read his rights and hauled off to the local police station.

Tom got the call that afternoon and flew down to Seattle the next morning. When Tom arrived, Cooper said nothing—whatever vestige of humanity he had left within himself was now subsumed by anger and bitterness. There would be no warm brotherly reunion, no apologies, no gratitude, and certainly no guilt. If anything, Cooper resented his older brother more than ever for having everything he never did—money, success, looks, a future. And most of all, Tom had been given something Cooper could never have—five more years with each of their parents.

After all that had gone down, it was obvious to Tom that his brother not only deserved prison time, but might actually benefit from it. He had escaped from military school but wouldn't escape from jail. And maybe, just maybe, the discipline, confinement, and structure of a few years behind bars might drive a wedge between Cooper and the fury that had consumed him all these years.

Ultimately, Cooper received a four-year sentence. Four years that were eventually reduced by five months as a result of good behavior. For a while, Tom suspected his brother of faking his suddenly civil demeanor, but over time he came to feel that Cooper's conversion was, happily, for real. Gone was the hatred and hostility. At long last, Tom had his little brother back.

At the same time Cooper was turning his life around, Tom was on the ascent as well. Business was good and he loved his work. He met and eventually married a Juneau-based architect named Lisa Tolliver and their son Jordan was born two years later. The marriage didn't work out, but the divorce was amicable. Lisa and Jordan moved to Vancouver, and Tom made sure to see his son as often as possible.

Seven years later—only a few months ago—Tom met a travel photojournalist named Claudia Hollister and within weeks, he spent as many nights a week in her nearby condo as in his own small house. In fact, marriage seemed inevitable and so right that they even discussed it on their third date. True to her empathetic nature, however, Claudia insisted that they wait on getting married until after Jordan's imminent visit this summer. After all, she reasoned, it wouldn't be fair to introduce the now ten-year-old boy to a "second mother" before they'd even had the chance to get to know each other first.

For all the positivity in Tom's life, though, one enormous disappointment had clouded the past few years. When Cooper was granted an early release, Tom invited him to stay with him in Caribou Bay for as long as he wanted. For a few months, the arrangement seemed to suit both brothers. Tom even got Cooper a job at a local hardware store, and for the first time in his life, the troubled young man seemed truly at peace with himself.

It didn't last long. One day in 2032, the hardware store's junior manager berated him for doing a "half ass job," and Cooper completely lost it. He picked up a shovel and bashed the guy's head in as the store's owner looked on in horror. Cooper was arrested for manslaughter, received a fifteen-year sentence, and was shipped off to the local prison. Over the past few years, Tom visited Cooper monthly but their relationship had seemingly been severed beyond any possible repair.

CHAPTER FOUR

On the only road from Juneau to Caribou Bay, there was a section where a narrow two-lane wooden bridge spanned a gorge below. On one side of the bridge, the road led downhill through forested terrain to the town in the distance. On the other side, the road wound its way higher up into the mountains.

A cargo truck was stopped halfway across the span of the bridge. The front cab had smashed through the wooden barriers on the right side of the bridge and the rest of the truck was at an angle covering both lanes. Though it was May, it wasn't uncommon to still find patches of snow and ice on the road.

Surrounding the truck was a four-wheel-drive vehicle marked Alaska Department of Transportation and an

SUV with an emergency bar across the top marked Caribou Bay Police. Standing off to the side was the truck driver, Matt Barlow, and next to him was Police Chief Teddy Newland. In his early forties and sporting a bushy mustache on a warm, amiable face, Teddy was a big guy who could easily pass for a football tackle.

Teddy put his arm on Barlow's shoulder and said, "You sure you're okay, Matt?"

"Damned if I know what happened, Chief. One second, I'm taking the bridge nice and easy, the next I'm seeing my life flash before me."

"Probably hit some ice. Damn lucky the rail stopped you."

"You got that right."

Teddy moved toward the damaged front cab of the truck, standing next to which was Ned Gray, a civil engineer wearing a Department of Transportation inscription on his shirt. Teddy gestured toward the broken section of the bridge, a gap about twenty feet across.

"What are we looking at?"

"Next week at the earliest," Gray responded.

"Can't you push it a little, Ned?"

"We need to do a retrofit this time, Teddy. Sorry, no one's driving to Juneau until at least next Tuesday."

"Damn. Okay, thanks, Ned."

Teddy walked back toward Barlow, then heard his cell phone ring.

"Newland." He listened intently for a moment, then said, "Alright, I'm on it." He put the phone back in his jacket pocket, then smiled at Barlow. "One of those days."

Teddy hurried toward his vehicle and sped off.

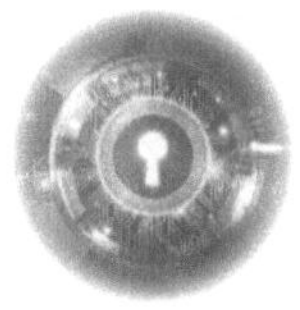

CHAPTER FIVE

Screaming sea gulls were circling over the picturesque town of Caribou Bay. Commercial boats dotted the half-moon bay, and in the foggy early morning light, vessels were weighing anchor and chugging out toward fishing grounds.

The piers were busy with fishermen repairing nets and boating gear, arranging crab and lobster traps. Two or three boats had been hauled out of the water and were being repaired or repainted in their cradles.

The harbor gave way to the town's main street, featuring a sign reading: Caribou Bay, Borough of Juneau, Pop. 2,540.

The street was small-town Northwest Frontier style, the buildings favoring regional design with a Gold Rush flavor. Just about every vehicle was either a four-wheel drive or a small truck.

On the main street, there was a bank, grocery store, convenience store, a few clothing stores, and several coffee shops with early customers wandering in.

The street was also home to Steiger's Hardware, Boating & Sporting Goods and a modest two-story office building displaying professional service plaques, including Mayor Orrin Parker, Attorney at Law, and Gene Lochman, MD.

Beyond the roofs of the town, log cabins and clapboard houses dotted the surrounding hills. The hills themselves were green with summer around the corner, but the background—dominated by spectacular peaks all around—was white and glacial as it often was even this time of year.

A few blocks off the main street was a residential area that included an attractive condo development.

Inside one of the units, an alarm clock started blaring. The jarring sound was emanating from Claudia Hollister's bedroom.

The offending alarm clock was alongside a double bed in which Tom, now thirty-eight, and Claudia, thirty-four, were suddenly jolted awake. Claudia reached over and silenced the clock.

"I want that clock dead," a half-asleep Tom muttered.

At which moment his cell phone rang.

"You too," he said to the phone.

Seeing who the caller was, Tom lifted the phone and said with a smile, "Make it good, Teddy. I'm asleep."

Claudia pushed out of bed and pulled on an oversized cardigan.

Tom turned to her and said, "Where are you going?"

She smiled lovingly and said, "Like you'd ever turn him down."

She knows me too well, Tom thought with a grin.

"What's up?" he asked Teddy. Tom listened and then added, "Okay, I'll call Harry, have him roll out the bird. Be ready in ten."

A few minutes later, a fully dressed Tom entered the kitchen and poured himself a mug of coffee. Claudia, very attractive with long amber hair, was at the table sipping her own cup of coffee and she handed him a blueberry muffin. As he took a bite, she asked, "What is it?"

"Chopper's down near Daniel Peak—all I know."

Tom pulled on a jacket as Claudia rose and snuggled next to him.

"Take care of yourself," she said.

"You sound like a wife."

"Just practicing."

Tom smiled, then said, "Don't forget Jordan's coming in today."

"If you're tied up, call—I can pick him up."

Tom grinned. "I don't deserve you."

She smiled and said dryly, "I know."

They moved into Claudia's living room and corner office area. On the wall were tacked several covers of "Alaska Monthly" magazine featuring Claudia's byline and photo credit. Also tacked up were photographs of Claudia and Tom in various rugged outdoor settings— river rafting, rock climbing, flying in Tom's chopper.

The images stirred precious memories in Tom's mind, along with the anticipation of countless new experiences yet to come. Truth be told, he had been resigned to a life alone after his marriage to Lisa had dissolved. It wasn't that he liked being on his own; in fact, Tom had no interest in turning into one of those lonely, scraggly-bearded recluses living out his days in some remote cabin in the vast Alaskan wilderness. Gregarious, warm, and intellectually curious by nature, Tom actually enjoyed being around other people and had been yearning for a meaningful relationship with a woman since he and Lisa went their separate ways.

The problem over the years after Lisa had been finding someone who shared his particular combination of passions and sensibilities. Someone who not only loved Alaska but wouldn't secretly be clamoring to escape the boundaries of a quaint, old-fashioned, decidedly slow-paced small town like Caribou Bay. Someone with a spirit of adventure who reveled in the wonders of nature like he did. Someone who could become a second mother to his young son and perhaps an actual mother to a future son or daughter. And someone who realized that two people on the same wavelength could speak volumes to each other without necessarily saying a word.

Fortunately, Claudia was all this and much more. Kind, compassionate, bright, talented, and beautiful, she was the kindred spirit he had been searching for all his life. And the fact that she felt the same way about him made his proposal of marriage on only their third date seem less of a surprise and more of a given.

A stunning woman by his side forever and a cherished young son en route for the summer. Life couldn't get any better than this.

"How's the Klondike article going?" Tom asked.

"Slow." She gave him a warm smile and then said, "Too many distractions."

Now both reacted to a car horn from outside. They kissed and Claudia said, "That's it—we're G-rated for a while."

"Jordan will be crazy about you."

"Don't rush it, Tom. We've got all summer. Give him time to adjust."

Tom nodded. She was right, of course. As usual. He gave her another quick kiss and hurried off.

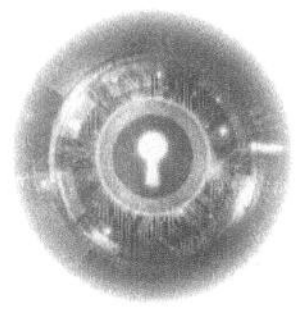

CHAPTER SIX

As Teddy's SUV was pulling up, Tom emerged from Claudia's condo and climbed into the passenger seat.

"Morning. What's the story?" Tom said as they drove off.

"It's your pilot buddy, Quine."

"Jimmy? What happened?"

"Flying some supplies back to the prison. Radioed in over Daniel Peak, then nothing."

"When?"

"Forty-five, fifty minutes ago. Search and Rescue's up and running. Warden thinks he may have run into some weather and went down."

"I don't know—Jimmy's too smart to fly in dumb weather."

"Charlie's meeting us at the airstrip with a survival pack. Let's hope we need it."

"Amen to that," Tom said.

After a moment, Teddy smiled and said, "Hey, Jordan comes in today, right?"

"Yeah, can't wait. But I'm still nervous."

"Him meeting Claudia? Hey, don't be. He's a bright kid; he'll see how right you guys are together. Only question is—when do I do my best man thing? Still September, right?"

"Ask my kid. Why do you think I'm so nervous?"

"It's nice to ask your kid. Just don't forget to ask *her*."

"Done deal," said Tom with a grin. "I mean, she loves Alaska, hates small talk, cries at the movies, puts up with me. Who else could I find like that?"

"Me, but you're not my type."

Ten minutes later, the SUV arrived at the Caribou Bay Airfield. The modest airport featured a few private planes on the tarmac, several corrugated hangars, and a "tower," which in reality was the glass-enclosed second story of a small operations building.

Another building the size of a large garage was off to one side of the airport with a sign on it reading: Brooks Helicopter Service—Tours, Instruction.

Outside the building was a Bell 206 helicopter, which at this moment was being fussed over by Harry Tyler, early fifties and perpetually, almost unnaturally, cheerful. A state of mind he had apparently been in since moving to Alaska ten years ago after being an aviation executive stuck behind a desk fifty hours a week in Dallas.

Teddy's SUV pulled up and both Tom and Teddy hurried out.

"Morning, Harry," Teddy said.

"Hey, Teddy. All gassed up and ready to go, Tom."

"Thanks. See you at poker tonight?"

"You *bet*," Harry responded with a smile, proud of his little play on words and clearly forgetting he had told the same "joke" at least twenty times before. Tom warmly returned the smile, grateful as ever to have such a sweet and even-tempered colleague on his team.

A police vehicle now pulled up and Sergeant Charlene Porter—a tall and striking twenty-five-year-old Native American—got out.

"Hey, Charlie," Tom said.

"Hi, guys."

Charlie opened the rear door as Teddy joined her. Together, they removed a weighty survival pack. Now

Harry opened the rear door of the Bell, took the pack from Teddy and Charlie, and stored it in the chopper.

"Good luck. I'm back on patrol," Charlie said, taking an admiring look back at the Bell, which she had flown three times already as one of Tom's best students. She exchanged waves with the others, then piled into her 4x4 and drove off.

Inside the chopper, Tom and Teddy buckled up and put their headsets on. Tom started the engine and a few moments later, the Bell reached altitude and soared off.

A short ride later, the helicopter was hovering above a postcard-worthy mountain summit, chiseled into which were several deep canyons. In the background, high-level ridgetops glared bright white with snow. Tom and Teddy continued scouring the region but saw nothing unusual.

"Damn," Teddy said.

On a hunch, Tom circled around another time and gazed down into one of the canyons. This time, he spotted a flash of metal at the base of the canyon.

"There!" Tom said as he pointed.

Moving closer, they could see the wreckage of a helicopter scattered across the bottom, at least 150 feet straight down from the summit. The canyon itself was narrow, just barely forty-five feet wide, surrounded on all four sides by sheer walls of rock and ice.

Teddy peered through his binoculars and could now make out the figure of Jimmy Quine near the wreckage. He wasn't moving.

"Tom, it's Jimmy. Not sure if he's alive."

"Only one way to find out."

Tom stared at the canyon floor, then at the chopper's blades, measuring. The only access to Quine was directly down between the rock walls, and the Bell's rotors would barely fit in this space.

Catching on to Tom's calculations, Teddy muttered, "Oh, shit."

"I can make it," Tom said. With Teddy looking over to him warily, Tom smiled and added, "I think . . ."

Teddy's eyes opened wide, but Tom was only concentrating on the descent to the canyon floor.

"If he's alive, he's probably in bad shape, Teddy. Got to risk it."

"Oh, joy."

Just then, Tom started inching the Bell slowly down toward the canyon like Santa Claus about to navigate the world's smallest chimney. A gust of wind suddenly caused the tail of the chopper to start dangerously bumping against one of the rock walls. Fighting the controls, Tom steadied the helicopter and lifted it up and out of the shaft.

"Okay," a relieved Teddy said. "On to plan B."

"Who said I'm done with plan A?"

And once again, the Bell descended into the canyon, the rotor blades coming so close they flicked grains of dust and avoided solid contact with the wall by only inches.

Expertly working the controls, despite particles of rock repeatedly smashing onto the chopper from above, Tom at last managed to navigate the canyon and hover in place just above Quine and the wreckage. Teddy then opened the passenger door, lowered a ladder, and climbed down.

Reaching Quine, Teddy checked his pulse and then gave Tom a thumbs-up. He then picked up Quine's inert body and, summoning every ounce of his strength, lifted him over his shoulder. At this, Quine briefly regained consciousness and weakly climbed the ladder with Teddy doing virtually all the heavy lifting. The added weight sent the chopper off balance, but Tom quickly compensated and kept the Bell as steady as possible under the circumstances.

In the cabin, Teddy set Quine in the front seat and belted him in, then he moved to the back seat, pulled up the ladder, and closed the door behind him. Quine's eyes closed, and he was once again unconscious.

The chopper then slowly rose. No easier going up than coming down, maybe harder. A steady stream of small rocks and dust showered the windshield, threatening Tom's visibility.

Five tense minutes later, the chopper at last emerged from the narrow shaft of the canyon. Inside, a smiling Teddy said into his headset, "You're good. You're *nuts*, but you're good."

Tom gestured to the sleeping Quine. "Yeah, 'cause he taught me."

Now Tom fiddled for a frequency and spoke into his headset: "Kamcheka Point, this is niner four two niner, come in."

An operator responded, "Kamcheka Point operational control, go ahead niner four two niner, over."

"Inform the warden we have Quine on board, but he's going to need medical attention. We're on our way. ETA five minutes. Niner four two niner over and out."

CHAPTER SEVEN

Tom's chopper angled down toward the secluded Kamcheka Point Federal Prison complex in the mountains and landed on a rooftop helipad. The rotors came to a stop and Tom and Teddy emerged.

There to meet them was Warden Sam Mulroon. In his late forties, gruff and gravely voiced, he showed the hard edge of a prison administrator. Mulroon was accompanied by a couple of prison hospital orderlies rolling a gurney. They hurriedly transferred Quine, again conscious and in pain, and rolled him toward the building entrance.

"Thanks. Coffee's on me soon as we get Jim settled," Mulroon said to Tom and Teddy.

"Don't thank me," Teddy said. "He did the flying—I did the praying."

As the three men followed the gurney, Teddy said, "Warden Sam Mulroon, Tom Brooks." Tom and Mulroon shook hands.

"You out of Juneau, Mr. Brooks?"

"No, Caribou Bay. You're new here, right?"

"Six weeks tomorrow. How'd you know? Jimmy tell you?"

Tom and Teddy exchanged looks. "No. Let's just say I've been here before, though it's been longer than usual. My brother's a . . . guest of yours."

"Is that right?" Mulroon said. After an awkward pause, Tom said, "Cooper Brooks, early thirties. Cell block C."

"What's he in for?" Mulroon asked.

Tom didn't appreciate the warden prying into his family business, but since the answer could be easily checked, he said, "Manslaughter. In fact, I was going to visit him again next week. Might as well do it today."

"Not visiting hours. But have them call me; I'll get you in."

"Thanks."

A short while later, Tom, Teddy, and Mulroon were in the prison infirmary, looking from the corridor past a partition. On an examining table was Jimmy Quine, stirring a bit, eyes half open. A doctor was finishing his examination, a couple of attendants alongside him. A few prisoners were in other beds.

The doctor exited the infirmary and joined the others.

"Looks like a broken wrist, few cracked ribs, concussion," the doctor said. "We'll know more after X-rays. He wouldn't have lasted very long out there."

Teddy squeezed Tom's shoulder—well done.

"Tom?" a weak-voiced Quine said.

"I'll catch up with you," Tom told the others.

Mulroon gestured. "Cafeteria's down the corridor, third left. We'll wait for you there."

Teddy and Mulroon moved off as Tom and the doctor approached a somewhat disoriented, clearly medicated Quine.

"Give us a second, okay, Doc?" Quine said in a whisper.

The doctor moved off and Quine managed a smile. "Thanks, Tom."

"What the hell happened, Jimmy?"

"Not sure . . . weird . . . guy running, then I'm down."

"What 'guy'?"

"How'd you get me out, Tom? I remember where I crashed. That must have been some piece of flying."

"Learned from the best."

Quine smiled. He reached out with his good hand, weakly clutched Tom's hand, then after a moment, was out. The doctor walked back to Quine's side and Tom headed to the door.

"Okay if I check back later, Doc?"

The doctor nodded and Tom left. He followed the infirmary wing corridor and took a left toward double doors at the far end. But he paused when he got there—wrong place. Then, before he could turn away, the double doors opened and two security guards emerged. Although they were wearing traditional prison guard uniforms, they had distinctive blue arm bands and ID badges that bore the name and logo: "GenQuest Bio-Tech."

At the sight of Tom, the guards assumed an all-business demeanor: "Help you?" the first guard said brusquely.

"Looking for the cafeteria," Tom said.

Just now, his eyes were drawn to the oddly modern room behind the guards. At the far end of the room was a huge metal door, the entrance to a vault-like structure. Tom could barely make out a color-coded sequential lock on the door, but more visible through a picture window next to it was an array of space-age equipment of indeterminate function.

On the vault door, Tom could see the words *GEN-QUEST BIO-TECH PROCESSING AREA. Restricted Entry.* All ultra high-tech and completely out of a place within a traditional prison complex.

The second guard quickly closed the outer doors as the first guard stepped closer to Tom.

"Back there and left. You'll see the sign. *Cafeteria.*"

Fine line between helpful and hostile, but Tom had no interest in a confrontation with either, much less both of the imposing guards in front of him, so he retreated to the main corridor where he turned left and the guards turned right.

A few minutes later, Tom poured himself a cup of coffee and settled at a table alongside Teddy and Mulroon.

"What's all that high-tech jazz down the corridor?" he asked Mulroon.

"High-tech?"

"Something called GenQuest Bio-Tech, whatever that is."

"Oh, new medical research program," the warden said dismissively.

Tom leaned in and smiled. "Tell the truth, Warden. You guys cloning J. Edgar in there?"

CHAPTER EIGHT

A half hour later, Tom watched with his usual blend of sadness and anger as Cooper was brought into the visitor room. It had only been a few weeks, but his brother looked five years older. Indeed, most people at this point would be hard-pressed to tell which of the two siblings had been born first.

A stone-faced Cooper took a seat and stared at Tom vacantly.

"How are you, Coop?" Tom asked.

"Still here, big brother."

"It's not forever."

Cooper produced a half smile.

"Jordan comes in today."

"You finally going to bring him to see me?"

"Not sure. He's meeting Claudia for the first time. Lots to adjust to."

"Doesn't matter. I'll see him soon enough. Like you said, I'm not here forever."

And with that, Cooper turned to the guard and waved him over. "I'm ready to go back."

"I just got here," a puzzled Tom said.

"Tired. See you when I see you."

Cooper stood up and was escorted out as a thoroughly perplexed Tom looked on.

CHAPTER NINE

As Tom was finishing his brief visit with Cooper, a car turned off Main Street in Caribou Bay and parked behind a building in a reserved space marked: "D. Steiger." Don Steiger, a burly fifty-year-old, exited the car, tooth-picking the remains of his lunch. He headed for the rear entrance of his store: Steiger's Hardware, Boating & Sporting Goods.

Steiger's was one of those old-fashioned mom-and-pop hardware stores that had seemingly been around forever—the kind that had been pushed aside by the jumbo chains in so many American communities. But, then again, Caribou Bay wasn't like most American towns. This was Alaska's answer to Brigadoon—a special place frozen in time that was in no apparent hurry to evolve much beyond its longstanding frontier origins.

Living up to its name, the midsize store was replete with tools, boating and fishing equipment, and dozens of bins filled with assorted hardware items. Ten or so customers and employees were milling about within, including a young man filling his handheld shopping basket with various bolts and nails. He nodded to Steiger—everyone knew everyone in this small town— who smiled and headed for a back office.

The young man was about to resume shopping when he paused, listening. Suddenly, there was a low humming, almost electrical, turbine-like sound, and with it, a wind. Now pennants started fluttering, price signs started waving, cardboard containers started flapping. Everyone looked around in confusion.

And then the wind picked up—but from where? It was wailing now, shooting around the room like an army of lost souls.

But what happened next wasn't merely confusing, it was downright terrifying. Everyone's attention turned to several bins lined up along a wall, all packed full of miscellaneous items like small tools, building materials, oarlocks, metal letters, aprons, and dish towels.

While the contents of the bins were all different, they all had something otherworldly in common—a forceful disturbance that gradually built from fluttering to a cyclonic whirlwind.

With dozens of objects flying through the air as if caught in some indoor tornado, customers and employees all started screaming, diving for cover and racing for exits.

At this, Steiger rushed out of his office and gaped in astonishment. Now his attention was drawn to another wall in the store that contained drawers and bins of smaller metal items. In seconds, tens of thousands of nails and screws and bolts and hooks went flying. The air was thick with chunks of metal whining like a beehive.

Transfixed, Steiger watched helplessly as a middle-aged woman dove into a protected niche, gasping as rakes, brooms, window screens, dishes, and flatware shot past her. A few feet away, an older couple was pressed into a corner, holding on for dear life as hammers, chisels, pliers, screwdrivers, planers, drills, and trowels sailed by and crashed all around.

Another customer, the young man who moments before had nodded to Steiger, dove behind a counter as a hunting knife soared toward him and just missed taking off his ear.

Now the glass in several displays exploded into a million pieces and the items within were sucked out.

Steiger turned to run back into his office when his forearm took on dozens of bloody tracks from the flying glass. As he ran, his shirt was shredded within seconds, his back lacerated as though from a thousand lashes.

Diving to avoid the incoming onslaught, Steiger managed to pull a display case in front of him as a shield, even as a pair of garden shears smashed into the case inches from him.

As a trio of sailing boat masts flew by like javelins, Steiger tried again to escape by diving for his office door, but it slammed shut before he could get there. Just now, a hunting knife thunked alongside his neck, missing by a hair. He tried desperately to open the door to his office, but it was locked.

And as Steiger looked on in horror, two axes whizzed toward him, almost parting his scalp. He let out a shriek and then saw a section of iron gating tipped with steel barks hurtling toward him. Frozen in terror, Steiger watched as the gate section smashed the office door open. He toppled within just as a squadron of saws flew past, one of them slicing into the base of his neck.

In front of the hardware store, passersby continued to race away from the cyclone inside as customers ran out screaming and windows exploded onto the sidewalk and street.

Meanwhile, in the alleyway behind Steiger's, two menacing-looking German shepherds were behind a fence guarding a locked lumber yard next to the rear of the store. Already howling because of the tempest underway at the hardware store, the dogs now reacted to the presence of a shadow moving along a wall across from the yard.

Their barking and growling soon reached an ear-piercing crescendo as the shadow continued past the yard toward the street beyond.

And then everything went quiet.

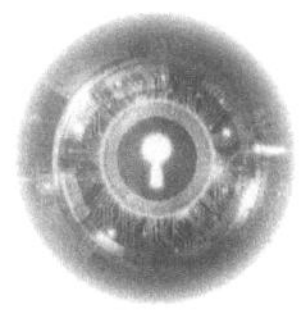

CHAPTER TEN

NOVOSIBIRSK, RUSSIA

A man who rarely slept more than five hours a night, Russian geneticist Dr. Sergei Baranov was wide awake in his home office at midnight when his email alert chime rang. Most of the messages he received these days were irritating little missives from his higher-ups in government checking for the millionth time on the progress of his work. He had learned long ago to ignore such bureaucratic wastes of his valuable time and was about to ignore this one, but then he saw it wasn't from his Moscow bosses at all. It was from his informant at GenQuest Bio-Tech in Alaska.

Baranov opened the email and read anxiously:

Doctor,

Something of monumental importance has occurred here related to Dr. Layton's experiments at Kamcheka. As you know, I am not directly involved with that particular program, and in fact have not as yet even seen our prison research facility, but word has spread here in our main office that one of the experiments has gone terribly, terribly wrong. Since you have asked me to relay all news, whether positive or negative, I wanted you to know I am doing my best to learn what has transpired in the obvious hope that the information can help you in some way, if only to avoid whatever setback has taken place. I will of course keep you fully apprised as soon as I learn anything useful. Please stand by.

Y

Tall, chiseled, and movie-star handsome, Baranov slammed his hand on the desk. A setback of any kind was the last thing he needed right now. The last five years had been defined by a seemingly endless series of setbacks and it was only a matter of time before the powers that be cut off his funding and possibly decided he himself was more of a useless liability than a valuable commodity.

It had all started going south, of course, five years earlier when the Americans authorized a midnight helicopter raid on a research facility he and the late US General Carter Prescott had set up at an abandoned Roscosmos space research complex in Siberia. Using prisoners for experimentation, Baranov had been on the verge of a medical and military breakthrough—the development of an easily transmissible form of TimeLock which would compromise the physical and mental acuity of enemy soldiers on the battlefield.

Although Russian President Antonov and his war-loving minions supported Baranov and the turncoat Prescott because they saw this new iteration of TimeLock as the ultimate non-nuclear weapon, the doctor and his American partner had a very different outcome in mind. For them, the goal was never to create a new Russian weapon, it was to create a new deterrent every nation would have access to—a form of chemical warfare so heinous *nobody* would dare use it. Conventional war's version of mutually assured destruction. A way to stop the madness of war before it even began.

It was an elegant solution Baranov believed in at the time. But the American raid five years earlier changed all that. That night, he not only lost some valued friends and colleagues, including Carter Prescott, he lost a woman who was serving as his research assistant and had just agreed to become his wife. The Americans had ruined his personal and professional future and had almost taken his life as well. Baranov's only objective now was to develop through advanced genetics a way to decimate Russia's enemies—something so powerful even American ingenuity would be at its complete and utter mercy.

Perhaps he would find the answer himself or perhaps his unknowing counterpart, Dr. Emory Layton in Alaska, would provide the breakthrough he needed thanks to his well-paid informant at GenQuest Bio-Tech. And with that thought in mind, a broad smile crossed Baranov's face. Because nothing would be more satisfyingly ironic than if his informant's intel proved revelatory, and it turned out to be American ingenuity that made such a breakthrough possible. No, that wasn't entirely true. Something else would be equally if not more satisfying than even that: eliminating the two people most responsible for bringing down Baranov's Siberian operation—Morgan and Janine Eberly.

CHAPTER ELEVEN

Teddy's SUV came screeching to a stop in front of Steiger's Hardware. Teddy and Charlie Porter hurried out and ran toward the storefront. Several dazed and slightly injured people were just outside or emerging from within.

Addressing everyone in earshot, Teddy said, "Doctor's on his way. Anyone seen Don Steiger?"

A few people shook their heads. Teddy rushed inside as Charlie tended to the injured. Once in the store, Teddy took in the aftermath of its utter destruction. It was as if the place had been ravaged by its own private hurricane.

"Oh, my God . . ." he said.

Now Teddy reacted to a groan as he neared the back of the store. He ran into the office and found Steiger lying on the ground, his neck and shoulder bleeding and the saw next to him. Teddy leaned down to him.

"Jesus, Don. What happened?"

Steiger could only stare, wide-eyed and frozen in terror.

CHAPTER TWELVE

Tom looked on anxiously as passengers who had just arrived on the flight from Vancouver filed through the gate at Juneau Airport. It had been longer than usual since he last saw Jordan—three months, as it happened. It was nobody's fault, really, just a confluence of circumstances—Tom's ex and Jordan staying with her parents in San Diego after her mother's knee replacement surgery, Jordan's school schedule, Tom's work.

But there was an upside—instead of the usual short visit, Jordan was being allowed to stay in Caribou Bay the entire summer. And Tom couldn't wait.

A few minutes later, a good-looking ten-year-old boy appeared carrying a zippered bag. Tom greeted him with a huge hug, but Jordan responded with minimal emotion—a far cry from his usual effusive demeanor.

"Hey, you look good," Tom said. "And grown. What are you, twenty-five now?"

Jordan barely managed a thin smile.

"Real proud of you flying here on your own! How was the trip?"

"Fine."

"What's in the bag?"

"Video games."

Tom waited for him to say more, but it didn't happen.

"Let's get your luggage."

On the tarmac a while later, Tom and Jordan walked past a couple of small planes and a maintenance hangar toward Tom's latest Bell 206. As they reached the chopper, Tom unlocked the cargo door and threw Jordan's luggage in. Jordan looked over the helicopter, clearly impressed.

"I traded up. How do you like it?"

"Um."

Tom smiled knowingly. Even a cranky Jordan couldn't hide his obvious interest in the new chopper.

A small van pulled up. Behind the wheel was facility supervisor Joe Bonner.

"Hey, Tom, who's your copilot?"

"This is my son, Jordan. Just in from Vancouver for the summer. Jordan, say hello to Joe Bonner."

Jordan nodded.

"Hi ya, Jordan. See you next week, Tom—I'll run the specs on your new hangar. So long, guys."

"Later, Joe," Tom yelled as the van drove off.

Tom and Jordan climbed inside the Bell and put their headsets on.

"This isn't one of your friendlier days, is it?" Tom asked rhetorically. Adjusting his earphones and microphone, Jordan just shrugged. Tom fired up the rotors and the Bell lifted off.

Zipping over the rugged Alaska coastline, Tom tried yet again to break the ice. "You did well at school last term. I liked your grades."

"I did okay."

"How's your mom doing?"

"Fine."

"This is a really thrilling conversation."

Jordan remained silent, arms disinterestedly crossed over his chest. Suddenly, Tom reached over to the control panel and flicked the autopilot switch on. With the Bell gliding along smoothly on autopilot, Tom folded his hands over his chest—mimicking Jordan.

"You mad at me or something?" he asked.

Jordan shrugged an unconvincing no.

"You realize when I was your age, I was twenty."

A dumb old joke that was usually good for something. Not this time.

"Tough room," Tom deadpanned.

With which he reached over and turned off the autopilot. The chopper started bouncing around and Tom folded his arms again.

"Tell you what—*you* fly."

Jordan's eyes opened wide. "Huh?"

"She's all yours."

A nervous Jordan tentatively took the controls.

"What—what do I do?"

"Same as you did on the old Bell."

Now the helicopter was wobbling and starting to vibrate.

"I need help, Dad!"

"Really?"

"Dad, please!"

"No fun alone?"

Jordan remained silent, but the answer was obvious. Tom took over the controls and steadied the Bell.

"Look, I know it's always a little weird at first—one minute you're the man in the family, then you have to be my kid again."

Jordan looked over in concession.

"And I know you keep hoping me and your mom will get back together. And I especially know you don't like the idea of me being involved with someone new, but nothing changes how much I love you. Okay?"

"Okay."

"So instead of 'fine' and 'um,' just talk to me. I'll always listen. You know that, right?"

Jordan let go a big smile and said, "Um . . ."

Tom returned the smile and said, "Now how about a little teamwork?"

Tom placed Jordan's hands back on the controls, then placed his own hands over Jordan's to work the controls together. They shared a smile as the Bell smoothly maneuvered through a series of turns and climbs.

Approaching Caribou Bay, Tom took over the controls. Jordan, his mood upbeat now, unzipped his bag, took out his phone, and started playing a song. In seconds, the formerly dour boy was gyrating as if he had just been transported to a heavy metal concert. Tom smiled and brought the Bell in for a landing.

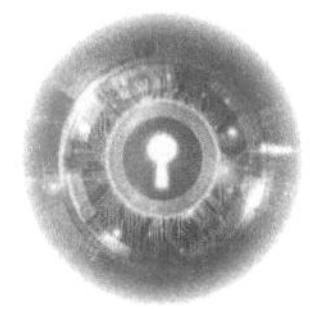

CHAPTER THIRTEEN

Tom's SUV pulled up in front of his cozy midsize house, in front of which was a large flat meadow-like area. The closest neighbor was a quarter mile away.

Inside, the house was wood-paneled with timbers and beams jutting across a high cathedral ceiling. The sense of the outdoors—of Alaska—was conveyed throughout. For Jordan, coming here was more than a little bitter-sweet—the home that was no longer home, the family that was no longer a family.

"Look in the closet," Tom said.

Jordan did so and took out a large, gift-wrapped box. He opened it to find a huge puzzle—a colorful map of Alaska. Jordan opened the puzzle and dumped out the contents—a thousand pieces.

"Used to do these with Uncle Cooper . . . only smaller," Jordan said. "How come he hasn't written me lately?"

"Maybe we'll visit him in a couple of weeks."

Jordan nodded, then gestured to the puzzle.

"You ever made one this big?" Jordan asked.

"Yeah—took me all summer."

They exchanged smiles.

"I wish we lived together all the time," Jordan said wistfully.

Tom moved closer and gave Jordan a big hug.

"Me too."

Jordan moved toward the mantle above the fireplace. On it were several photos, including one of Tom's parents standing behind two young boys, one thirteen, the other eight. Tom's father was wearing his Alaska Airlines pilot uniform. Another photo showed Tom at nineteen, posing next to his fourteen-year-old brother on a fishing pier. A third photo depicted Tom in the pilot's seat of a chopper.

And a final photo showed Tom and Claudia, both in hiking outfits.

Seeing Jordan react to the last photo, Tom said, "Her name's Claudia. She's a writer and photographer. Moved here from Juneau last year. You'll meet her later."

"I thought maybe you and Mom . . ."

"Jordan, it's just not going to happen. Mom and I want different things out of life. But there's one thing we agree on completely—we both love *you*."

Jordan smiled, then gestured to Tom and the two sat on the floor and started working on the puzzle.

Later that night, with Jordan sound asleep in the guest bedroom, Tom was in the middle of his weekly poker game. Also playing were Teddy, Harry Tyler, and Mayor Orrin Parker, who had earlier told the others on the phone the good news that Don Steiger was on the mend and had even heartily encouraged them to play cards and not worry about him.

"The miracle is nobody else got hurt or killed," Teddy said.

"Anybody figure out what happened?" Tom asked Teddy.

"Tom, nobody in this world could explain what I witnessed in there. You saw the footage from that customer's phone. I mean, maybe if the whole town got hit, but the inside of one store? I've got a dozen witnesses and none of them ever saw anything like it in their lives."

After a long, thoughtful moment, Tom finally looked at his cards and said, "Check."

"Whaddya say, hizzoner the mayor?" Teddy asked Orrin.

Orrin quietly shoved a pile of chips over. Teddy dropped several chips in the pot.

"I'll see you and raise a quarter."

Harry studied his hand and folded. Now Tom looked over at Teddy, smiled and said, "Why do I love him? Look at that dopey face. The man's been bluffing his ass off since high school and I still can't beat him. Fold."

Teddy returned Tom's smile and said, "You get the girls, I get the cards. That's the way of the world, son."

With which he laid down three jacks. Orrin tossed in his cards as Teddy collected the pot.

"Deal me out one," Tom said as he got up from the table.

"Where the hell is Art?" Orrin said. "This isn't poker, it's solitaire."

Tom went into the guest bedroom where Jordan was asleep, a video game joystick still in his hand. Tom freed the joystick, shut off the game, kissed Jordan on the forehead, and pulled up the covers.

Tom returned to the poker table with a pensive look on his face, just as Teddy was showing his latest winning hand—a full house.

"Sorry, fellas," he said as he raked in his chips.

Orrin, only half in jest, threw down his cards and grumbled, "Teddy, next hand like that, I'm back to banging a gavel and you're behind bars."

As Harry started dealing, Teddy reacted to Tom's introspection.

"What is it?"

"Don, of course. I mean—what in God's name could possibly account for what happened there? And Jordan. He just got here, and all I think about is how tough it's going to be when he leaves."

Teddy patted Tom on the back warmly, then picked up his cards and let go a big smile. One of those nights.

* * *

At this very moment, Officer Art Bickford, a recently relocated Texan in his early thirties, was seated at his desk at the Caribou Bay Police Station. The phone was ringing and he picked it up.

"Caribou Bay Police. Officer Bickford speaking. . . . Motor vehicle registration? This is the city police, sir. You might want to try the Department of Motor Vehicles in Juneau in the morning."

He hung up and shook his head—dumb call.

* * *

Back in Tom's house, Teddy was collecting his latest pot when Tom's landline phone—still a necessity due to spotty cell phone reception in the area—started ringing.

"Hello? Oh, hi, hold on. Teddy, it's Art at the station." Teddy took the phone.

"Hate to bother you, Teddy, but some guy's raising a ruckus over by the lifts."

"What do you mean? The lifts are closed."

"Yeah, well, some kids say this guy got 'em going. Broke into the generator room, trashed some stuff, powered up the lifts, and took himself on a ride up the mountain. They think he's still up there."

"Damn. Okay, I'm on my way."

Teddy hung up and grabbed his jacket.

"Something strange is going on at the ski lift. Give me twenty minutes and keep that seat hot."

"Nobody can fill it like you, buddy," Tom said.

Teddy smiled and headed out.

CHAPTER FOURTEEN

Although skiing season was months off, the ski areas above Caribou Bay were stunning as usual. Teddy was never much of a skier, but he often came up to this glorious mountain setting to enjoy the dual view—Caribou Bay just below and seemingly every star in the universe just above.

Tonight, the silent ski lifts dangled over forested dales, running up to a peak set in sharp relief against a bright moon. Teddy drove up, parked, and got out to look around. It didn't take long for him to spot a storehouse with the door smashed in. He moved toward it and took in a pile of shovels and other items scattered about.

And then a sudden instinct prompted him to look up toward the mountain peak at the top of the lift he was standing nearest to. There in silhouette was an unusually tall male figure, his features unclear.

"Come on up, Ted," a basso profundo voice beckoned.

Teddy's eyes opened wide. Not only did this person know his name, but his voice was clear as a bell despite emanating from hundreds of feet above.

And now Teddy was jolted again as the ski lift suddenly cranked into action.

"What the hell you think you're doing?" Teddy yelled. "Get down here!"

Just now, huge rocks started crashing down all around Teddy, and he quickly ducked behind the storehouse. Even in the darkness, he could tell that the rocks were coming from the mountaintop. The figure was somehow hurtling them down like an otherworldly hailstorm.

Several rocks began to smash into the storehouse, coming within inches of hitting an incredulous Teddy. He took out his cell phone, but one of the rocks crashed directly into his hand and crushed the phone to pieces.

* * *

Down to three, the poker game had been suspended. Tom and Harry were watching television as Orrin played solitaire. The phone rang and Harry said, "Whoever it is, see if he wants to play."

Tom smiled as he picked up the phone. "Hello?"

He listened for a moment and then his expression turned grim.

"What! Oh, no. Damn . . . thanks for calling, Gene."

Tom hung up the phone and looked over to Harry and Orrin.

"Steiger . . . he didn't make it."

"But Doc said he was on the mend!" Orrin said.

"Not sure it was just physical. The poor guy was traumatized to death."

"What's going on here, Orrin?" Harry asked, but the mayor could only shrug.

The group went silent for a minute until the sound of the doorbell jostled them back to reality. Tom went to the door and opened it to find a grinning Officer Art Bickford.

"Sorry I'm late, guys. Deal me in."

Now Bickford noted everyone's expression.

"What?"

"Art, Dr. Lochman just called," Tom answered. "Steiger's dead."

"Oh, shit," Bickford said. "But I thought he was getting better?"

"We all did."

Bickford looked around the room. "Where's Teddy?"

"He took off," Tom said. "Checking on that ski lift business."

"What ski lift business?"

"Don't know—*you're* the one who called him about it."

"Not me. I haven't spoken to Teddy since late afternoon."

"Jesus, Art, I spoke to you too."

"Tom, I'm telling you, it wasn't me."

"Something stinks. Let's check it out." Tom turned to Harry. "Look in on Jordan, will you? Be back as soon as I can."

"Sure thing," Harry said as Tom and Bickford headed out.

* * *

At the ski lift, Teddy was still behind the storehouse but easing out now that the rock attack had stopped. He quickly moved into the open and headed for the now operational ski lift.

After jumping on a passing lift chair, Teddy unholstered his gun, clicked off the safety, slid a round into the chamber, and reholstered the weapon.

Halfway up and just over a deep gorge, Teddy was stunned to hear the same deep voice sounding close enough to be in the seat next to him. "Come on, Teddy. Come get me."

He looked up to see the same figure, still silhouetted against the moon atop the ski run.

At the same moment, Bickford's car sped into the lot at the base of the ski lift. Tom and Bickford jumped out, then peered up the mountainside.

"Teddy? You up there?" Tom shouted.

"I'm here!" Teddy shouted, and a split second later he reacted to a loud clunking sound as the lift came to an abrupt stop. And then the ski lift started to quiver—a gentle shaking at first that gave way to a violent shudder. As if a giant hand were shaking it.

At the base, Tom and Bickford reacted to the quivering cables. A panicked Bickford shouted, "What the? . . . Earthquake?"

"The ground's not shaking," Tom said. "It's only the *cable*. Got any glasses?"

Bickford, however, was frozen, unable to answer or move. Tom ran to the vehicle and found the binoculars. He ran past Bickford to get closer to the base of the lift, looking around frantically for a control mechanism to bring Teddy down.

Tom focused the binoculars on Teddy's lift, now vibrating wildly some two hundred feet above the ground. Teddy was clutching the safety bar for dear life. And then Tom and Teddy reacted in horror as the ski chair stopped shaking and then turned completely upside down.

Teddy wrapped his arms and legs around the safety bar to keep from falling just as the chair started shaking wildly again. And through the whistle of the wind, a chilling laugh could be heard.

On the chair, the safety bar was secured by a steel plate and four thick bolts. But now the bolts began to turn, as though by some huge unseen wrench. In a matter of seconds, three bolts unscrewed and fell free. Now just a single bolt held the safety bar in place as Teddy stared down to the floor of the ravine, where a stream, silver-sheened in the moonlight, cut through the canyon below.

Just then, the final bolt turned, the plate wrenched free, and Teddy began the long fall to the dark gorge below.

"No!" a shocked and horrified Tom shouted. Then, aware of movement high above, he raised the glasses again to see an imposing figure, the face broad and high-cheeked, the skin a taut steel-gray color that was almost luminescent in the moonlight, the short-cropped hair as silvery as tinsel. There was a metallic solidity to the figure, the shoulders large, the torso solid but narrow-waisted.

The rising moon cleared the trees and splashed the figure in an eerie light. His eyes intermittently flashed, as though pulsing with some unearthly energy. Bathed in shadowy moonlight, a huge smile appeared on his face.

As Tom continued to watch in astonishment, the figure turned and started running along the ridgetop with immensely long, graceful strides until it disappeared amidst the trees.

In the gorge below, Teddy's pulverized body was sprawled across a boulder. The stream lapped at one outstretched hand. His dead eyes stared at the night sky. Headlights played across his face.

A shaking Bickford approached a devastated Tom.

"What happened up there, Tom? Jesus Christ. What happened?"

Too numb to offer an answer even if he had one, Tom simply stared at the gorge below and then back to the ridge where whomever—or whatever—he had seen vanished into the night.

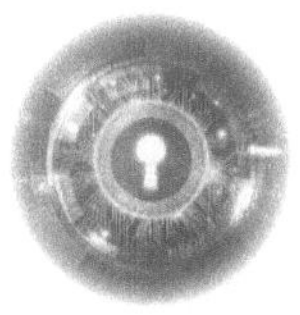

CHAPTER FIFTEEN

Under a full moon, the expanse of Alaska's Juneau Icefield was especially breathtaking—a rugged 1,500-square-mile bed of glacial ice with a surface dominated by jagged ridges called seracs.

Straight ahead in the distance was Mendenhall Glacier, most often partially obscured by a perpetual fog-like haze hanging over areas of the icefield.

On the south end of the icefield was a quarter-mile of forested land, while to the northwest, the forested area gave way to cliffs marked by a series of waterfalls.

Anyone taking in this all-natural splendor would have been shaken to suddenly notice the decidedly unnatural sight of the figure looming up and moving in a north-eastern direction into the forest.

In the forest, he headed for an abandoned cabin located almost a quarter mile from the southeastern edge of the icefield. The night sky was spotted with heavy clouds, and at this altitude, there was still plenty of snow on the ground.

Wearing a one-piece coverall, he paused before the cabin door. His eyes flashed, and the door opened by itself.

Inside the cabin, the figure flicked a light switch. But nothing happened. He smiled and then, as if on command, the lights shone from two old lamps. The cabin hadn't been lived in for years, but had been kept up nonetheless. The furniture was all covered and a few skins were tacked to the walls. Draped over a sofa were prison clothes.

The figure wandered, then stood before a faded and cracked mirror. He touched his face and reacted with a combination of astonishment and disbelief. And then—satisfaction.

With an almost childlike eagerness, he moved to a chair before the fireplace, took off the protective cover, sat down, and closed his eyes. His deep concentration soon began to manifest itself as half-burned logs and charred embers suddenly burst into flames.

Smiling throughout, he concentrated again and then the prison clothes flew directly into the roaring fire. And then all the protective covers lifted up and were blown away out a window that opened and then closed. A radio suddenly turned on and a country western song was playing.

After a few moments, though, the music faded into the background as the figure stared intently into the fire and the murky and indistinct holographic image of two men and a woman materialized out of the swirl of fire and smoke.

He stood and faced the image.

"Hard to believe, I know . . . but it's me—only new and improved. Better than anything you ever thought I could be. Better than anyone's ever been before. I don't know what I am anymore," he said while raising his arms in messianic triumph, "but I *like* it."

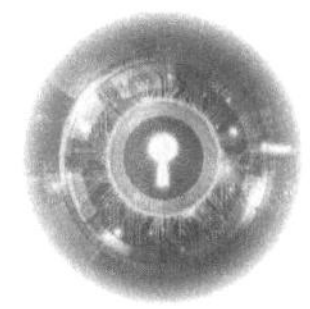

CHAPTER SIXTEEN

Tom's SUV pulled up in front of Claudia's condo. Tom and Jordan got out and headed toward the entrance.

"Tom, I'm so sorry about Teddy—I loved him too," Claudia said quietly as she opened the door. She quickly adjusted her demeanor as she looked at Jordan.

"And this handsome young man must be Jordan."

"Jordan Brooks, Claudia Hollister," Tom said.

"Glad to meet you, Jordan."

"Hi," an expressionless Jordan said.

"Come on in," Claudia beckoned.

Tom leaned toward Claudia. "This isn't how I wanted you guys to meet. I'll be back as soon as I can. Hope you don't mind."

"Of course not."

Jordan remained stone-faced, then Claudia gestured toward her computer, which featured an especially large monitor she used for her photography work.

"Ever played Shark Fest 2039?" Claudia asked.

"No."

"It's all set up. What do you say we try it out?"

Jordan shrugged an unenthusiastic acceptance, then spoke the word that had long ago become the universal expression of youthful indifference: "Whatever."

Claudia, however, had the perfect comeback and said, "Nobody I know has ever gotten past the second level."

And with that, Jordan was suddenly interested. Claudia smiled as he moved toward the computer and settled in front of the monitor. She went to the game's introduction page.

"Jordan, why don't you look this over for a sec and I'll be right back."

Tom and Claudia moved toward the kitchen and she gave him a long hug.

"Thanks," said a visibly shaken Tom.

"What's going on, Tom? On the phone—"

"I said his death wasn't an accident, and it wasn't."

"What then?"

"I saw someone . . . something. It killed Teddy and it must have killed Steiger too. Just don't go anywhere, and don't let Jordan out of your sight. The bridge is down and a storm is headed our way. Otherwise, I'd get the two of you as far away from here as possible."

Claudia's eyes opened wide, but for Jordan's sake she remained silent. Tom started toward the front door, then looked over to Jordan, excitedly playing on the computer.

"See you later, Jordan! Have fun."

Jordan smiled and waved without looking at Tom.

"Tom, I'm scared," Claudia said.

"You should be."

CHAPTER SEVENTEEN

A half hour later, Tom and Officer Art Bickford were at the uppermost point of the ski lift. They examined the disassembled chair, which had been rotated to the top. Though not on the police force, Tom found himself far more focused on the investigation than Bickford, who was clearly thrown by the entire business. It was understandable, given what happened, but Bickford was a cop and it was time to tend to the job at hand.

"Tom, you don't really think—I mean, it had to be the wind."

"It wasn't the wind."

Tom trudged on in search of clues as Bickford apprehensively followed. A few yards farther, Tom stopped and leaned over to examine a shallow patch of snow. In it was a partial footprint, including distinct sole cleats.

Tom knelt down to take a closer look. Left foot. Large foot size. He stood up and continued walking until he spotted another partial print. Right foot. Tom studied the ground—there were no prints in between. His eyes narrowed in astonishment. The running stride was approximately ten feet. Impossible.

"Jesus Christ," Bickford said as he dropped to his knees and searched the ground. "There's gotta be prints in-between," he said, his voice wobbly.

"See any?" Tom responded.

Bickford rose, measured the distance with his own stride.

"It's three steps at least!"

"This is his normal running stride. I saw him. He wasn't doing a broad jump, he wasn't pole vaulting, he was just running. Nice and easy."

Bickford stared in astonishment.

"What are you going to do, Art?" Tom asked. "Art?"

* * *

"He *quit*?" Mayor Parker said to Tom in his law office an hour later.

"I'm not sure I blame him, Orrin."

"That's great. Now I'm down to just Charlie Porter."

"Orrin, soon as anyone can get here, you have to get some backup from Juneau."

"Tom—you sure about this? I mean, Teddy. You said yourself it was dark—"

Tom shot him a look.

"Oh, shit," Orrin said.

CHAPTER EIGHTEEN

At fifty-five, Leland Gaines was a contented man. His years as a big-league prosecutor in Seattle and then in Juneau had made him feared, respected, and wealthy. And right this minute, he was enjoying the fruits of that success fishing in a stream adjacent to the upscale log cabin in Caribou Bay where he and his wife spent most of their summers.

The day was crisp and clear, and, at this height, there was still snow on the ground. The fish had been biting sporadically, so he'd try again after lunch. He gathered his gear and headed back toward the charming cabin they had bought ten years earlier.

Inside the cabin, Paula Gaines was preparing a hearty meal of soup and sandwiches. Affectionately, she watched her husband making his way home and yelled out, "How'd it go?"

"Great . . . for the fish," he shouted back.

She smiled and went back to getting their lunch ready. Had she still been watching her husband, however, she would have noticed what he now saw in the final seconds of his life as the snow on the ground in front of him began to stir, creating tiny whorls of movement. And then the snow started to sink and swirl like a wildly spinning funnel, creating a larger and larger whirlpool into which everything around it was sucked, including Leland Gaines.

Gaines tried to scramble in panic. But the widening sinkhole was overtaking him. His movements grew ever more sluggish as the suctioning crater clutched at one foot and then the other, sucking him down into a seemingly bottomless vortex. Gaines was disappearing with a strangled cry.

And it was at this very moment when Paula looked outside and let out an ear-piercing scream as she watched her husband disappear forever into a cyclonic pit that hadn't been there thirty seconds before.

CHAPTER NINETEEN

Inside Orrin Parker's office, Tom was ready to head out when the mayor's secretary, Diane Reid, burst in.

"Charlie Porter just called. It's about Leland Gaines—"

An alarmed Tom and Parker quickly rose and the oblivious Diane said, "Why is everybody so jumpy today?"

Twenty-five minutes later, Tom's chopper, Tom and Orrin inside, fluttered into view and settled near the Gaines's cabin.

As they emerged, Tom and Orrin both stared in awe and bewilderment at the funnel-like crater into which Gaines had disappeared. A dozen or so vehicles dotted the area and nearly as many volunteers were digging into snow and earth, attempting to find Gaines as his wife—his widow—cried hysterically in the background.

Charlie Porter rushed up to the chopper as Orrin got out and closed the door. Tom, still checking instruments, kept the rotors on idle.

"Nothing yet," Charlie said. "We're down about ten feet." She hurried off and Orrin nodded glumly.

Tom was just about to shut down the engine when something caught his eye—the same mysterious figure. Far away, but discernible.

Tom hit the controls and lifted off as Orrin looked on in surprise. Tom again spotted the figure, now standing astride an outcropping of rock atop a high ridge, hands on hips, legs apart. Then he turned and disappeared among the rocks.

Tom flew closer—close enough to now see the figure running easily up an incline. Moments later, the helicopter was directly above him and then slowed to match his running speed—fifty-six miles an hour! Tom wanted to take out his cell phone and capture this impossibility on video, but the dangerous terrain made it too risky. In fact, just now he had to carefully maneuver the Bell through multiple snowy ravines and gullies just to keep up with the creature, or whatever it was, running below.

And then his quarry was gone, lost somewhere amidst a seemingly endless series of rocky passages. So Tom lifted the chopper to higher ground and sheer crevasses leading to a serpentine canyon. With a clearer view, Tom was now able to get a better look at the figure below, again perched triumphantly on a ledge. Tom already knew he was big and muscular, but now it was evident that he was human as well. And yet, not quite.

Hovering one hundred feet off the ground, Tom was now eye level with the creature that had taken his best friend's life, and they stared at each other for a long moment in silence.

Suddenly, a down draft lowered the craft ten feet and moved the rotor blades to within inches of the ledge on which the figure was standing. Here and there, the canyon wall started to crack as the vibrating chopper engine sent loose dirt falling. A few seconds later, the ledge crumbled and gave way, causing the figure to tumble, arms flailing.

His left arm hit the scissoring rotors and was instantly severed near the shoulder.

After struggling with the controls, Tom set the Bell down and shut off the engine, prepared to get out. But his attention was then drawn to his quarry, the face more metallic than the night before, the hair a brighter silver. The figure rose, looked at the gaping wound where his arm was severed and—working on nothing more than instinct—began concentrating intently, eyes flashing.

Just now, a reddish glow—an admixture of blood and God knows what else—seemed to congeal on the stump of the arm. A silver-gray substance formed. And it pushed out like a growth, because that's exactly what it was: the severed arm was being replaced. Within seconds, it was full grown, extended to normal length. A new hand moved, new fingers flexed. Regeneration!

Tom blinked—can't be. And then the figure stared at his new arm. Trying it out, he extended his elbow and moved his fingers around. Perfect. He beamed, dazzled by his own performance, euphoric with the attainment of raw, boundless power. Then he looked at Tom and raised his newly restored arm to the sky in proud triumph. As Tom reacted in shocked fury, the figure smiled, then suddenly sprung away with catlike power, taking off as though shot from a gun, up and across a huge boulder and out of sight.

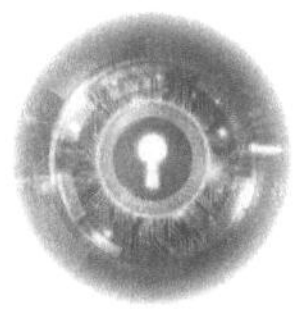

CHAPTER TWENTY

Back in his office, Mayor Parker was seated at his desk, opening a small package. He pulled out a brand-new nine-millimeter automatic with a bright gold handle. Several clips were in a see-through plastic bag. He took a clip and jammed it into the gun.

Tom entered the office, spotted the weapon, and said, "Put it away—it won't help."

He closed the door behind him and locked it. After a thoughtful moment, Tom looked at Orrin and said, "Teddy, Leland Gaines, Steiger—their deaths are all related."

Orrin put the gun in the desk drawer. "What do you mean 'related'?"

"Orrin, we've got to move fast."

"You're not making sense, Tom."

"Listen, I don't know what he is or what he wants, but whatever it is, it's not good. And something else—this is crazy, but he looked familiar."

Orrin's eyes opened wide.

"Call the governor, Orrin. Get the National Guard. The bridge is down. Tell them to come by air—storm or no storm—and do it now!"

"Whoa, boy. I still don't know the facts here."

"You're not a judge anymore trying a case, Orrin," Tom said impatiently. "You want facts? Whatever 'he' is, he lost an arm to my chopper. The blades cut it off—and he grew it back again. Right in front of me."

Orrin stared, his eyes blinking his disbelief. His lips moved, but all that came out was incredulous silence. Until: "How could that be? That's impossible."

"Not for him."

"Tom, are we talking . . . *alien* here?

"I don't know. I don't think so. Despite everything, there's something too . . . human about him. He's more like some kind of—mutation."

"I don't understand."

Tom thought for a moment. Then it hit him. "Gen-Quest Bio-Tech! Ever hear of it?"

"Yeah. Some kind of medical research company, I think. Set up shop here a few years ago. Why? What's the connection?"

"Maybe nothing . . . maybe everything."

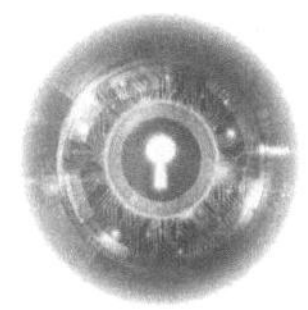

CHAPTER TWENTY-ONE

The rain was beating down now, but it took much more severe weather than this to slow down everyday life in Caribou Bay. A couple of fishing boats were unloading their crab catch at the docks. Here and there, townspeople in slickers wandered the shops of Main Street.

At Nellie's, customers were enjoying a hearty American lunch, everything from hot dogs to burgers and fries. There was also an open rotisserie with three chickens on the skewer.

Several teenagers were noisily wolfing down their meals when the figure entered. His imposing size and odd appearance of course attracted everyone's attention. If anything, his skin tone had again changed to a more metallic hue.

All conversation immediately ceased. The figure moved before the kid behind the counter and pointed to the rotisserie.

"Give me those," he said.

"I just put 'em on. Need about fifteen minutes," the trembling young man said.

"I don't think so." His eyes flashed, and instantaneously, the three chickens were individually wrapped in rings of fire.

As several customers bolted out and a few others who remained shakily pointed their phones to take videos, the chickens were singed and roasted in a flash. Then, one by one, they slid off the skewer and into open takeout cartons. The cartons promptly closed and flew toward the visitor, landing on the counter before him.

Next, the french fry basket lifted up and emptied its load of fries into another carton. A salt shaker and ketchup bottle lifted from the counter, levitated, and then poured out their contents onto the potatoes. The carton closed and then hovered over to the figure.

"How much?" the figure said.

The kid behind the counter was still gaping.

"How *much*?"

"Fifteen seventy-five?" came the tremulous answer.

With that, the cash register dinged open and three fives and a single lifted out and slapped into the young man's hand.

"Keep the change."

CHAPTER TWENTY-TWO

Driving in his SUV through heavy rain, Tom took the long and perilous mountain road up to Kamcheka Point Federal Prison.

Arriving at the employee housing area, he got out and knocked on unit 33A in one of the newly built wood structures.

"Come on in, Tom," said Quine from inside.

Tom entered the modest but comfortable unit to find Quine in a jogging outfit, several bandages wrapped around his forehead, rib cage, and wrist. He was sitting in an easy chair next to a telephone table. As Tom moved toward him, Quine remoted off the TV. The two men shook hands.

"You look good," Tom said.

"I look like shit, but thanks. Drink?"

"It's not a social call, Jimmy. I need your help."

"Sure. And Tom, I'm so sorry about Teddy. You guys were like brothers."

Tom's head drooped down, and he realized he hadn't really had time to process the loss yet. Not just that Teddy was gone forever, but the gleefully satisfied look on his killer's face that would haunt Tom the rest of his life.

After a moment, Tom took off his rain slicker and hung it on a coat tree near the door before sitting in a chair near Quine.

"What do you know about GenQuest Bio-Tech?"

"I fly, I don't pry."

"I'll take anything you've got."

"Even though I'm the security supervisor here, they don't tell me everything that's going on. I wish I had something to give you. Bunch of white coats and lots of big-ticket equipment. I think the company's based in Caribou Bay, but they set up some kind of remote facility here three or four months ago. That's all I know."

"In the sick bay, when I asked you what happened, you said something about a guy running. . . ."

"Yeah, that's right. Up on the ridge. Running real fast. I remember angling toward him. Next thing I know, the rotors stop. I don't mean they slow down, they just stop, and that's all she wrote."

"This guy—tall, strong, silver hair?"

A surprised look crossed Quine's face. "Yeah. You nailed him. I thought I imagined the whole thing!"

"You didn't imagine it. I've seen him too."

"And there's something else," Quine said. "I'm pretty sure he was wearing prison garb."

Tom's eyes opened wide. "A favor, Jimmy. I need to see Mulroon. Now."

Quine reached for the phone.

Fifteen minutes later, Tom was in the warden's office, which was institutionally furnished with a floor-to-ceiling window overlooking the prison complex. Tom was seated across from Mulroon, who was behind his desk. The warden's face registered alarm and astonishment.

"That can't be. I heard they were freak accidents."

"You got the freak part right, Warden. But the way they died was no accident."

"But what makes you think there's a connection to GenQuest Bio-Tech?"

"The question is, do *you* think there's a connection?"

"Of course not. I told you—they're conducting an experimental medical program in disease prevention."

"That didn't look like a country doctor's office down there. You sure there's nothing else going on?"

"It's out of the Justice Department, sanctioned by Washington, completely above board. What more can I say?"

"Why here?"

"Because the company is based in Caribou Bay and because we're the best equipped to oversee the program."

"And the 'patients'?"

"Strictly volunteer prisoners. In return, they're up for early parole. The federal prison system has been involved with volunteer medical experiments since the building of the Panama Canal. Your brother Cooper was one of the volunteers. You can ask him yourself."

This was news to Tom. "He never mentioned it."

"Probably he didn't want to get your hopes up. Getting out early, I mean."

"So he's getting an early parole?"

"No. Turned out he wasn't a suitable test subject. What is it you're looking for?"

"Maybe something went wrong with one of the volunteers."

"Not possible."

Tom stood up. "Are you stonewalling me, Warden?"

Mulroon hit an intercom buzzer and a guard immediately entered.

"Escort Mr. Brooks out."

Tom walked out, the guard in tow. After they left, Mulroon took out his cell, pushed a button.

"Emory, we have to talk, right now."

A few minutes later, Mulroon entered the GenQuest Bio-Tech control room, loaded with high-tech computers, monitors, and other sophisticated equipment. Several doctors and technicians were present.

The room featured a large picture window. At the window was Dr. Emory Layton, who, in his late sixties, made for a distinguished and grandfatherly presence.

Mulroon joined Layton at the window, where both men watched several MRI-like tubes with see-through glass canisters gliding along a magnetic rail. Designed for human occupants, the canisters slid toward a processing chamber. Within each canister was a strange haze. Once this phase was complete, the canisters glided into a processing chamber, where they were then hit by an incredible barrage of light and multi-colored rays.

Layton began evaluating data on a computer screen.

"Shut it down, Emory," Mulroon said. "It's out of control."

* * *

A few hundred feet away, Tom was standing in front of Cooper's solitary cell. Quine had called in to security to allow for the unplanned visit.

"How are you, Coop?" Tom asked.

"Just peachy, big brother. Weren't you just here two days ago? Or was it three? You know how time flies around here."

"Why didn't you tell me you volunteered for that GenQuest Bio-Tech program?"

"So you could talk me out of it?"

"I don't even know what it is."

"They radiate you or something—try to boost the immune system. What do I know? Told me I was the wrong blood type. My luck, right?"

"Do you know any of the men who did go through the program?"

"Just one. Frank Kaden. Three-time killer. Real sweetheart of a guy."

"Which cell block is he in?"

"The big cell block in the sky. He's dead."

"How?"

"Tried to escape from the lab. Made it to the ice-field, but they cornered him and he drowned trying to get away."

"What if he didn't drown?"

"What are you talking about? And why do you care?"

"There's something going on here. Listen, Coop—I'm going to ask to have you transferred to another facility."

"Nothing doing, bro. I leave the other guys alone here and they leave me alone. I'm not starting over somewhere else. Hey Tom—I'm tired. Let's wrap this up, okay?"

"Okay, but this conversation isn't over."

"You talk all you want. I'm taking a nap."

Cooper retreated to his bed and a concerned Tom headed out.

CHAPTER TWENTY-THREE

It was around 8:45 that evening when Tom's SUV pulled up in front of Claudia's condo. The storm was especially intense now, adding another full hour to Tom's drive from Kamcheka.

Claudia opened the door and gave Tom a big hug and kiss.

"I'm so glad to see you."

"Me too. You guys all right?"

Claudia nodded.

"Where's Jordan?"

Claudia took Tom's hand and led him toward her bedroom. She opened the door to reveal Jordan asleep on the bed.

"He really wanted to wait up for you."

Tom smiled, then closed the bedroom door. He then gestured toward the computer.

"We need to go online and check out a company called GenQuest Bio-Tech."

He sat in front of the computer, pushed some keys. Nothing. An internet provider logo appeared in the center of the screen along with the words Unable To Connect. Tom and Claudia tried their cell phones— same result.

"Damn," said Tom.

"We'll have to try later. Tom, what's going on?"

"Whoever . . . whatever killed Teddy, Gaines, and Steiger has something to do with Kamcheka and some kind of space-age research project."

"Isn't that where your brother is?"

"Yeah. I just saw him. I want him out of there. And I'm getting you and Jordan out of here as soon as I can."

"Tom, what is it? What's going on?"

"There's a creature out there, Claudia. He could have killed me, but he didn't."

"*Creature?* Tom, what are you talking about?"

"I'm not sure yet." He gestured to the computer. "That's what I'm looking for."

Dejected, Tom settled on the sofa. Claudia followed him and started massaging his shoulders.

"Tom, what aren't you telling me?"

"It's all so crazy. Just give me a few minutes. I'm still trying to put it together."

"You're exhausted. Let it go for tonight."

Claudia leaned in and smiled.

"What?" Tom said.

"What else? I love you."

"I love you too."

He pulled her in and kissed her. Then she rose and asked, "How about a sandwich?"

"Sure."

She walked into the kitchen, opened the fridge, and pulled out some ham and cheese.

"Tom, whatever's going on, let the police handle it. Okay? Tom?"

No response. She put down the food and headed back into the living room to find Tom sound asleep on the sofa. Lovingly, Claudia pulled off his boots, went to a cabinet, and took out a couple of blankets. She covered Tom, lay down on the carpeted floor next to the couch, and covered herself with the other blanket.

CHAPTER TWENTY-FOUR

Very early the next morning on a street near the northernmost part of Caribou Bay, a guard with a tranquilizer gun was speaking into a walkie-talkie.

"Hamilton Street. All clear. No sign of him."

At a nearby park, a second guard—also holding both a tranquilizer gun and walkie-talkie—was on patrol.

"Bay Park. Clear here."

A quarter mile away on a residential street, a third guard was standing next to a four-wheel vehicle marked: KAMCHEKA POINT FEDERAL PRISON. He looked around anxiously.

And two miles from him, another Kamcheka Point four-wheeler was parked in front of a small gas station at the end of Main Street.

Rounding out the team was yet another prison vehicle, this one being driven by Warden Mulroon with Dr. Emory Layton in the passenger seat. Both men were looking out the window intently, trying desperately to see through the ongoing rainstorm.

"Where the hell is he?" Mulroon asked.

"We'll find him," Layton said confidently.

"And when we do, you really think tranquilizers will be enough to hold him down?"

"Sam, don't you understand? We have a scientific miracle out there."

"No, Emory. We have a monster out there."

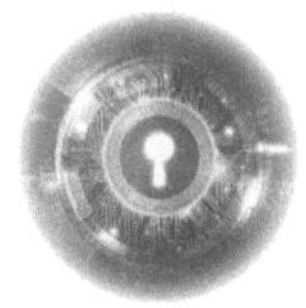

CHAPTER TWENTY-FIVE

Inside Claudia's condo an hour later, Tom and Claudia were seated in front of the computer. Internet access had been restored during the night despite the continuing bad weather.

Tom typed in the name *Frank Kaden* and the words *Alaska. Convicted murderer.*

"Who's Frank Kaden?" Claudia asked.

"My brother said he was one of the GenQuest Bio-Tech volunteer prisoners, then he escaped and was killed."

"And?"

"And I'm not so sure he's dead."

"I don't understand."

"Remember I said this creature looked not only human but familiar? Now I'm thinking maybe I saw him one of the times I went to visit Cooper."

"You think this Frank Kaden might be our . . ."

"Creature? Could be."

"But how?"

"I don't know. Damn. Nothing here about Kaden. I'll have to ask Orrin or Charlie Porter. One thing I'm pretty sure of, though—all roads lead back to Gen-Quest Bio-Tech."

Tom typed in the company name and the site came up. The home page described the company's founding five years earlier and mission to modify human genetics to better combat disease. On the bottom of the page was a corporate address only a mile away.

"I thought you said they were based up at the prison."

"No. The headquarters is right here. But they needed to set up shop at Kamcheka because that's where the so-called 'volunteers' are."

Now Tom went to the About Us page, where he and Claudia read the bio of Dr. Emory Layton.

"There's the man I have to talk to. I think I'll pay him a visit this morning."

Now Tom reacted with surprise. "Wait a minute—I know this guy!"

He directed Claudia's attention to the photo and bio just below Layton's.

"Yoshi Ito. Senior VP. Been with the company since it was started in DC. Brother-in-law of two-time Nobel nominee Dr. Louis Garrett. Moved to Caribou Bay three years ago when the company relocated. Why is he so familiar?"

"Maybe you took him on a tour in the Bell?"

"No. I don't think . . . Got it! I met him because of you."

"I've never seen the man in my life."

"You weren't there. He was trying to book the Bayside Inn for his wedding reception on the exact same Saturday night in September that I was. I was there first, so he took another weekend. Sweet guy."

"So maybe you start with him instead of going to Layton?"

"Maybe."

"And do you know this other man too?" Claudia asked, referring to the one other executive on the page: Victor Yullen, thirty-two, a senior technologist who had joined the company when it relocated to Caribou Bay.

"No clue."

Tom clicked on the site's News page, on which were links to a dozen or so press releases. Among the titles: "GenQuest Bio-Tech Founder Honored," "GenQuest Bio-Tech Relocates to Alaska," and "GenQuest Bio-Tech Readies New Alaskan Research Program."

Tom clicked on the last headline and a press release appeared dated eight months earlier:

GenQuest Bio-Tech, a leading medical research company, has entered into an agreement with the Department of Corrections to test a new medical process through the use of volunteer prisoners in Kamcheka Point Federal Prison near Juneau, Alaska. The company's founder, Dr. Emory Layton, claims the new genetic acceleration process shows hope of boosting the rate at which human anti-bodies combat a number of diseases . . .

* * *

Tom shook his head.

"What?" asked Claudia.

"Nothing there. Exactly what the warden told me. Except . . ."

He broke off in midsentence to open the bedroom door to check on Jordan, peeking in and finding the boy sleeping soundly.

"Except *what*?" Claudia said impatiently.

"I'm doing this all wrong. Thinking like a pilot. Too damn logical. The trick is to get inside his head. What's he after? He killed three people—what did they have in common?"

"Caribou Bay?"

"More than that. Teddy, Steiger, Gaines. How are they connected to each other and, if I'm right about him, how are they connected to Frank Kaden?"

Tom rose, moved toward the door, and put his coat on.

"Where are you going?"

"Orrin. Check out his files, maybe put it together. Listen, you and Jordan get over to my house. Plenty of room to land the chopper there. Soon as I can, I'm getting you both out of Caribou Bay."

"Not without you."

Without answering, Tom squeezed her shoulder and walked out the door.

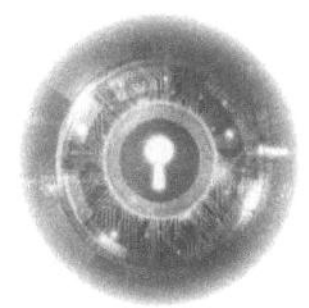

CHAPTER TWENTY-SIX

Tom had driven all of a hundred yards when his cell phone rang. He looked at the screen and answered. "Charlie, you okay?"

"Listen, Tom. I tracked our friend Kaden down. You were right—he's alive! And he was just spotted about fifty miles north of here, possibly headed to Haines."

"How? The roads are closed."

"He's not on a road. He's on a fishing boat on the Mendenhall River. Stole it, of course, but there were witnesses."

"Meet me at the chopper."

"Tom, this is a police operation. Let me call in help."

"Fine, but I'll get you there faster."

"On my way."

Ten minutes later, Tom and Charlie lifted off in the Bell 206 and soared over Caribou Bay and its neighboring valleys and mountains.

"You were right again," Charlie said into her headset.

"About what?"

"Getting me there faster. You're the only one—"

"Dumb enough to fly in this weather?"

"I was going to say brave enough."

"Not sure it'll pay off, though."

"He can't go far in a crappy old fishing boat on a river."

"That's the problem, Charlie. Why would a guy who can do what he can do *need* a crappy old fishing boat in the first place? And why would he suddenly hightail it out of Caribou Bay when he could just as well take over the entire town completely?"

"Yeah, I was wondering all that myself. Plus, he hardly matches the description you gave the mayor."

"I know. None of it makes sense, but Kaden's our only lead, so we have to get to the bottom of it. What did you find out about him?"

"Drifter. Triple murderer. Affiliated with a series of violent motorcycle gangs. Killed a group of fellow drug dealers four years back. Got life, then volunteered for that program up at Kamcheka. Didn't work on him—or at least that's what the warden claims—so no reduction in his sentence. But it was easier for him to escape from the lab than from his cell block, so he did. Mulroon swore he died in the icefield."

"But nothing directly connecting him to our victims, right?"

"Right."

"And nothing connecting him to me?"

"You?"

"Yeah. For some reason, our monster or whatever he is seems especially fascinated with me. He not only keeps sparing me, but he keeps taunting me. But why?"

"Why don't you ask him yourself?"

With this, Charlie gestured to the Mendenhall River below. Sure enough, the stolen fishing boat was making its way upriver. Tom lowered the helicopter and swooped down just above the boat.

Over the chopper's loudspeaker, Charlie said, "Frank Kaden. This is the police. Pull your craft to the side of the river and disembark with your hands in the air."

The boat promptly swerved to the side of the river and the man on board secured the old fishing boat to the dock. But instead of turning himself in, he disappeared from view for a second, then reemerged on a small motorcycle. Within seconds, the bike was speeding past the dock, over a small road and into the woods.

"Damn," yelled Tom as he turned the chopper to follow.

Kaden expertly raced through the woods as the Bell gave chase just above the tree line. More than once, Charlie covered her eyes and braced for the inevitable crash, but Tom was every bit as skilled as a pilot as Kaden was as a motorcyclist.

Fifteen terrifying minutes later, Tom said, "I know where we are now. Ready to end this?"

"Depends on what you mean by 'end'!"

Tom gave her a half smile, then lurched the helicopter ahead and even lower to the ground. Five feet at most now separated the tops of the tallest trees from the belly of the Bell.

Now Tom gestured to the mic Charlie still held in her hand. She handed it over and Tom said, "Kaden. When you get to the dirt road ahead, go right and you'll find a campground five hundred feet ahead. Stop your vehicle there and get out with your hands up or we start shooting."

"Tom, I can't fire into a public campground," Charlie said.

"I know. Don't worry, if my guess is right, you won't have to."

Just now, Kaden reached the small dirt road and sped off to the left.

Tom smiled with satisfaction, saying, "We've got him now."

Finally clear of the forest, Tom was now able to descend farther, and moments later, he and Charlie spotted their quarry. Kaden was at the end of the dirt road and looking around helplessly. Not only was the spot surrounded by tall hills he could never climb on the bike, but just beyond the end of the road was the top of a huge waterfall above a small lake that connected with the Mendenhall River.

Tom landed the chopper on the dirt road and both he and Charlie rushed out. Kaden got off the motorcycle and looked around like the trapped animal he was. He started to reach into his coat pocket, but Charlie—gun pointed right at him—shook her head.

"Don't do it, Frank."

With which Kaden dropped the gun to his side.

As Charlie moved toward her prisoner, Tom shouted, "Why did you kill them, Kaden? What did Teddy and the others ever do to you?"

Kaden gave Tom a puzzled look. "Who?"

"And why not me?" Tom yelled.

"You're crazy, man," a panicked Kaden shouted. With Charlie quickly closing in on him, Kaden suddenly bolted to the edge of the hill and plunged himself over the side into the avalanche of water raining down on the lake below.

"Shit!" Charlie shouted as an equally frustrated Tom ran up to join her. For a full five minutes, the two stared wordlessly at the waterfall and lake below, but Kaden was nowhere to be seen.

And then a new realization set in. If Frank Kaden was their monster, he might have just taken the answers to Tom's questions to a watery grave. Or if he had just used his advanced powers to survive the fall, he was more motivated than ever to use those same powers to wreak deadly vengeance on the inhabitants of Caribou Bay before.

CHAPTER TWENTY-SEVEN

The next day, at the lumber yard behind Steiger's Hardware, the figure approached the same guard dogs he had passed after the assault on the store. As before, the dogs started barking and growling fiercely. But this time when he stopped in front of them, the dogs suddenly froze in abject terror, then turned tail and ran off, yipping and whining.

He smiled broadly, then walked another block before leaping thirty feet to the top of a building.

Spotting movement on a nearby rooftop, two Kamcheka guards stationed at the park walked closer, then gasped in shock as they saw the figure spring some forty-five feet from one rooftop to the next, as if competing in some supernatural decathlon.

One of the guards looked down at his tranquilizer gun and said, "Screw this!" He put the tranquilizer gun in his jacket and pulled out a semi-automatic.

Just now, Tom's SUV raced up in front of Parker's office. And an ever-broader smile crossed the figure's face.

Inside the SUV, Tom shut off the engine and was about to get out. But the door wouldn't open. He pulled up the door lock lever, but it went right down again. He tried it once more, but the same thing happened. Then Tom heard the back door slam shut and the vehicle suddenly began moving. He tried applying the brakes, but to no avail.

Tom turned around. The figure in the backseat was smiling. And Tom could tell right away that he had changed since their last encounter: the silvery sheen of the hair was more pronounced, the skin had taken on a richer metallic gloss, and the eyes were farther apart by several millimeters.

"Nice day for a joyride," he said.

The SUV suddenly shot ahead at head-snapping speed. Tom's instinct was to fight the wheel and stomp the brakes, but it was useless. Then he looked on in shock as the car raced out onto a long pier.

"You'll kill us both!" Tom yelled, but his passenger just continued to smile. The SUV then crashed through the barrier at the end of the pier and dove toward the water. But instead of splashing in, it remained just above the surface, skimming along rapidly like a hovercraft.

In the back seat, the figure seemed to be having the time of his life. Realizing it was pointless for him to hold the steering wheel, Tom let it go and whirled around.

"What are you?"

"Don't ask too many questions. You may get in over your head."

Now Tom looked forward again. And for all his cool, his mouth parted as the SUV slowly slid beneath the waters of the bay and angled down, then leveled out and soared forward.

Somehow, though, the interior remained sealed—not a drop of water seeped into the vehicle. As the figure beamed with joy, Tom stared in astonishment at an underwater world that somehow seemed as alien as another planet in another galaxy.

"Here we go!" the figure said excitedly. And within seconds, the dense, colorless onslaught of water began to brighten.

A minute later, the SUV shot out of the water like a Polaris missile and headed toward cliffs overlooking a cove. The misty cove was impassable from its right side, but there was a rocky access to the next beach on its other side.

The SUV sailed through the air, then twisted around in midflight to face the water from which it had just emerged before touching down on the edge of the cliff. So close to the edge that it was slightly teetering.

Tom looked uneasily toward the boulder-strewn cove far below. Even as he did, the vehicle teetered ever more precariously forward. The figure climbed into the passenger seat next to Tom and said, "Enjoying the tour?"

"Different. You got any other trips planned? I'm still paying for this thing."

"You don't take me very seriously, do you, Tom?"

The SUV teetered further.

"You catching on, Tom? Attitude puts me on edge."

The figure grinned at his own joke as the SUV's nose inched even steeper. Inexorably tipping down now, the vehicle at last began to plummet and Tom braced for the crash.

But as it neared impact, the SUV slowed and straightened out only feet above the sand, then glided down to a soft landing. The driver's side door opened and a wobbly Tom jumped out.

The figure emerged and watched the frightened and angry Tom with delight.

"What do you want!" Tom shouted. "You're Frank Kaden, right?"

"Who?"

"Kaden. Out of Kamcheka. Remember the waterfall yesterday?"

"Afraid you've got the wrong man there, Tom."

"Then who the hell are you?"

"A mover and a shaker, that's who," he answered buoyantly.

He then turned toward the misty sky above the cove and his eyes flashed. An area of mist began to swirl and move only a few feet from where he and Tom were standing. Then the mist began to congeal and take shape, forming the images of two young boys, about twelve and seven. Tom stared, struggling toward recognition, but it wasn't there yet. Then he reacted, stunned.

"Okay, we're playing mind games—you got me and my brother, a day at the beach. What's the point?"

The figure moved closer toward Tom. "The point is . . ."

And then he took a long theatrical pause.

"It's me and *my* brother, too, Tommy."

Tom's face tumbled to shock. The figure grinned broadly, immensely pleased with his bombshell.

"*Cooper?*"

"In the flesh, big brother. Or something like it."

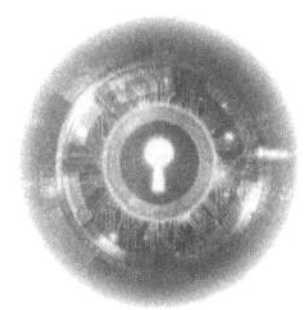

CHAPTER TWENTY-EIGHT

Cooper raised his arms in a triumphant pose and said, "Take a good look, Tommy. Is this up from the minors, or what?"

"I don't understand! I just saw you yesterday in your cell."

"You mean this?" Cooper said as a lifelike image of himself as he formerly appeared took shape next to Tom.

"Meet my stunt double, Tommy."

"But how . . ."

"After our little underwater adventure, you really think *this* was difficult?"

"You were in the GenQuest Bio-Tech experiments, weren't you? I thought you didn't qualify."

"Is that what they told you?"

Tom pointed to the "other" Cooper. "That's what *you* told me."

"Oh, right. Well, what can I say? I lied. You know that old advice: Never volunteer for anything? Dumb advice."

"Then you sent me on a wild goose chase after Frank Kaden too. Why?"

"I had work to do first. Actually, the work's not done, but I couldn't wait any longer."

"For what?"

"For *this*, of course. For my big reveal."

"You sick bastard! You killed three men. You killed my best friend!"

"They all deserved it, big brother. Why can't you see that?"

"All I see is a monster."

"That's all you've ever seen, isn't it, Tommy?"

Realizing anger would only inflame Cooper more, Tom forced himself to soften his expression. He moved closer to his brother.

"Listen to me, Cooper," Tom said as he gestured to the misty image of the two boys. "We can't go back to that. But you're still my brother. Whatever it takes,

I'll help you. Whatever they've done to you—maybe it can be undone."

"Are you out of your fucking mind? Get with the program, my friend. I'm a revolution."

Dust and sand began to swirl all around. A great column of sand soared upward, and Tom protected his eyes as the sand spun around his head. As the sand began to clear, Tom wiped his eyes and became aware of a beaming Cooper looking up. Tom followed his gaze up to a gigantic sand statue the size of the Statue of Liberty of—what else?—Cooper.

"You getting the picture, Tommy? Nothing like me has ever happened before. Am I right or am I right?"

Cooper looked over to the materialized "boys," both of whom were now clapping and cheering for him.

"I guess I'm right!"

"No—you get the picture, you freak! You're nothing but a cold-ass killer," Tom shouted.

"Shut up!"

A rain of sand began to fall as the reverberation from Cooper's rage caused the immense statue to crumble. Tom backed away as the image of the boys started to disintegrate, the mist dispersing into the air. Then the ground trembled as the great statue fell. At last the sandstorm cleared, and the cove returned to normal, all of the manifestations gone. Tom moved toward his brother.

"If you can do anything you want, then do something good instead of killing people."

"Killing them *is* something good. I told you—they deserved it."

"Teddy Newland arrested you because you killed somebody. He was only doing his job. And that's all the others were doing."

His anger mounting, Cooper said, "Your 'best friend' tracked me like a dog. Steiger couldn't wait to take the witness stand. And Leland Gaines prosecuted me like I was a serial killer."

Tom paused for a moment—thoughts swirling in his head, all leading to one obvious conclusion.

"Right you are, Tom," Cooper said, clearly reading his brother's mind. "Judge turned Mayor Orrin Parker put me away, and soon I'll put *him* away. I'm saving him for last, but I have a bit of unfinished business out of town first."

"What unfinished business? Where?"

But Cooper just smiled.

"Don't do it, Cooper."

Cooper just smiled and started to turn away.

"You going to kill me too?"

"Don't think I haven't been tempted. I've lived in your sanctimonious shadow my whole life. The golden boy and his loser little brother. You got all the glory and I got all the shit. Guess those days are over now, right big brother? So no, I'm not going to kill you. I'd much rather keep you around and watch you live your life in *my* shadow for a change."

Cooper ran off, his stride quickening. In seconds, he was leaping the rocky divider toward the next beach. Tom jumped into his SUV. It coughed and sputtered, then finally started, but was still bogged down in the sand.

Tom engaged the four-wheel drive and started rocking the vehicle until it finally broke free. As he drove off, he took out his cell phone but there was no signal. He threw down the phone and drove off to the adjacent wide beach and then onto a dirt road leading to a paved road above the beach where he gunned the SUV forward.

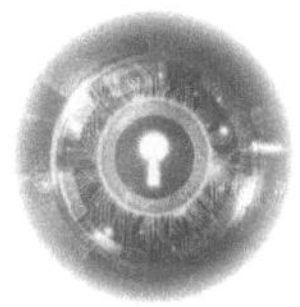

CHAPTER TWENTY-NINE

It took only fifteen short minutes seventeen long years ago to change the trajectory of young Cooper Brooks's life forever. That was the night when he realized his path was clear and his fate was sealed.

Looking back on the lead-up to that fateful night as he made his way to the desolate little town where he grew up, Cooper realized the one constant in his life had always been a desperate need for respect and adulation. But instead of being the center of attention, he was forced to feel like a guest star in his own life rather than the lead. All because the bright hot spotlight had been saved for an older brother who seemed put on this earth solely to make him look inferior by comparison.

So Cooper decided around the time he turned twelve that the only way he could stand out from his older brother Tom was to become very good at being very bad.

And, truth be told, Cooper Brooks simply wasn't wired for "good" anyway. Toeing the line, staying the course, being on the straight and narrow—not really his style.

As a result, by the time Cooper was thirteen, he had graduated from petty juvenile crimes like painting graffiti and stealing candy to selling pot and lifting wallets from tourists. That year, he hated Tom, he hated life, and he hated himself. But other than his father, there was one person Cooper didn't hate—Ellie Fernell. A year older than him, she was beautiful, funny, smart, and sweet. In other words, everything Cooper would never be.

Oddly enough, although Cooper was brave enough to repeatedly break the law, he was never brave enough to ask for Ellie's phone number. But for reasons he still didn't understand to this day, she approached him one afternoon and, with a maturity that seemed far beyond her fourteen years, asked him to take her to a school picnic. Of course, Cooper eagerly accepted. So eagerly, in fact, that he agreed way before she even finished the question, prompting her to teasingly laugh at him in a way that would have driven him to rage if it were anyone other than her.

For three glorious months, Cooper and Ellie were inseparable. The relationship was relatively chaste, but he didn't mind—just being in her company was gratifying enough. And like the juvenile idiot he was, Cooper actually believed they'd be together forever.

Unfortunately, after a while, Ellie's apparent attraction to a social outcast bad boy like Cooper passed. She found an older kid to hang out with, and on an icy winter morning that still haunted him even now, he was, in every possible sense, left out in the cold.

And then came the "incident." One day, another thirteen-year-old named Kevin Ibby asked Cooper to join him and his friends to practice shooting cans near the lake.

Fascinated by guns all his life, he said yes. That afternoon, Kevin showed him how to use the weapon, and holding it in his hand almost became Cooper's first serious sensual experience. Unfortunately, the nominal leader of Kevin's little band of troublemakers was a dick of a fourteen-year-old named Zeke Wilson. For whatever reason, he took an instant dislike to Cooper and within minutes he was teasing him relentlessly. Even seventeen years later, Cooper could still hear him laughing and calling him a skinny loser who couldn't shoot straight if his life depended on it.

He really shouldn't have said that. Not while Cooper was still holding a loaded pistol. Surprisingly calm, he turned toward Zeke, pointed the gun at him, and said, "Why don't we find out?"

Zeke's face turned ashen, but obviously he thought Cooper was just posturing. What he didn't know—and what Cooper himself didn't know until that second— is that he not only had it in him to fire that gun, but that he wouldn't lose a minute's sleep that night if he shot him straight through the heart.

Regrettably, however, Zeke was right about one thing—Cooper was a lousy shot. So when he aimed the gun at a tree near Zeke and pulled the trigger just to scare him, he accidentally hit the kid in the leg. It wasn't intentional, but when Zeke started screaming over his dopey little flesh wound, Cooper found myself laughing at him just as he had himself been laughed at minutes before.

Naturally, the other kids gathered around their fallen idol, Zeke, and Cooper ran home. Two hours later, the local sheriff came to the Brooks's house and thirteen-year-old Cooper was arrested and hauled off to juvenile detention.

As Cooper learned later on, that afternoon his dad went to Zeke's house and begged his parents to drop the charges. After all, their son was underage and playing around with a loaded weapon. Plus, Cooper's father agreed to pay for Zeke's medical bills and arrange for him and his parents to fly free anywhere in the United States on Alaska Airlines. They agreed and the matter was settled.

Cooper expected a big-time scolding from his father and, sure enough, he was immediately grounded for the summer. But somehow Cooper's dad saw something redeemable in his youngest son, even when nobody else possibly could. Maybe he knew the boy was still tormented by his mother's death even three years later. Or maybe he realized that screaming and yelling at Cooper would only further fuel the rage that had come to define him.

All Cooper knew was that his father was more interested in helping him than punishing him that fateful night. He knew his son's issues went far beyond one or two isolated incidents. He knew Cooper was, for whatever reason, nothing like his uncomplicated older brother. He knew what he needed wasn't anger, it was love.

And it worked. For the first time in Cooper's life since losing his mother, he actually felt remorse. Not so much for his petty acts of criminality, but for letting his father down. Because if Cooper Brooks ever truly loved anyone in this world, it was him. And it was time to prove it. He promised he would change, and he meant every word.

After their long talk, Cooper's father gave his son a big hug neither wanted to end. It did end, though. And then everything went wrong. One hour and fifteen minutes later, Cooper's one and only hope for redemption crashed and burned and nothing was ever the same again.

CHAPTER THIRTY

Damn it, Orrin, you're a sitting target if you stay in Caribou Bay!" Tom shouted at the mayor. The two men were in Orrin's home and Tom had spent the last half hour briefing His Honor on his otherworldly reunion with Cooper and how his brother now had his sights on the mayor.

"Listen, Tom—you've told me some very fanciful things here. Flying cars, holographic images, hundred-foot sand sculptures . . . it's a lot to take in."

"Take it in, Orrin. It's all true."

"Well, perhaps."

"We've been through this already. And haven't you seen enough with your own eyes to know what Cooper is capable of? You believe what you want, but you damn well better believe you're next."

"You think I'm not scared, Tom? But I'm the mayor. What am I supposed to do—sashay out of town and leave everyone else at his mercy? Besides, between the bridge and the weather, how could I leave anyway? Then there's this—if what you've just told me is true and your brother is, what, a thousand times more powerful than we originally thought, how could I possibly stop him from getting to me anyway?"

"You get every bit of firepower in this town to protect you—every cop, every rent-a-cop, every security guard, every reservist—all of them round the clock until we can bring my brother down. And I'll stick with you every step of the way. If I'm in the line of fire, Cooper might just leave you alone."

"Unless he turns on you too."

"Which is a distinct possibility."

"Okay," said Orrin. "That all makes sense. I'll make the calls and gather up a volunteer team. You said Cooper told you he had some—how did you put it?—unfinished business out of town? That might buy us a day or so."

"I just wish I knew what he was talking about. Either way, though, you have to alert every town and city in the region immediately."

"Will do. Let's just hope they heed the warning faster than I did."

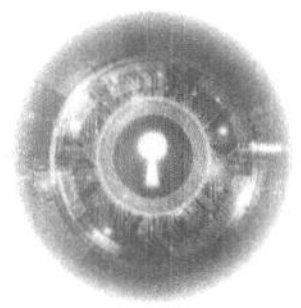

CHAPTER THIRTY-ONE

At the precise moment Tom was castigating Orrin for not hightailing it out of town, Cooper was already miles away from Caribou Bay in the small community of Talkeetna, where he and his brother had grown up. His first stop would be the most satisfying, but the second actually made even him—despite his seemingly boundless powers—a little nervous.

Cooper was hardly surprised that a misfit like Zeke Wilson—the little shit who had laughed at him and called him a loser when they were teenagers—had never escaped the confines of a tiny town like Talkeetna. A brief amount of research had shown that Zeke now worked at the Matanuska Valley Federal Credit Union, so that's where Cooper now headed.

Peering in the window of the credit union office, Cooper quickly found Zeke. The years hadn't been kind to him and Cooper delighted in his old nemesis's jowly face and pronounced stomach. But it was Zeke's hearing and not his appearance that was on Cooper's mind. Looking directly at Zeke, Cooper concentrated intently and the reaction was instantaneous. Zeke was suddenly hearing the sound of loud laughter surrounding him from all sides—a sound nobody else in the office could hear.

Cooper smiled sadistically as Zeke gazed around the office in confusion before finally rising and rushing out of the building as his befuddled coworkers looked on. Zeke covered his ears but the laughter continued to engulf him. Desperate for some kind of escape, he made his way to his car and climbed inside. The vehicle then sped off as Cooper ran alongside the road, hidden by the bushes.

Now Cooper focused again, and the volume of the laughter grew even louder. He could see Zeke screaming helplessly as he drove, his driving getting more and more erratic with every passing moment. As Zeke approached a small bridge, Cooper's voice suddenly permeated the interior of the vehicle.

"Remember me, Zeke? Cooper Brooks. You made fun of me when we were kids, and I should have shot you in the head instead of the leg. Well, look who's laughing now!"

Zeke's eyes opened wide in terror, reacting not only to what he'd just heard but to the fact that in his panic he had just crashed into the side of the bridge and was falling to the river below.

Cooper looked on victoriously as the car hit the ground. After a minute, Zeke managed to crawl out and slither to the river bank. Cooper considered finishing him off then and there, but decided leaving Zeke no doubt traumatized for life was even better payback.

Thirty minutes later, Cooper was hiding in the shadows behind a small gift shop owned by none other than Ellie Fernell—the girl a young Cooper had "dated" before she called the relationship off. Funny thing, though, Cooper couldn't bring himself to hold a grudge against her. In fact, he wasn't here to exact revenge at all. He was here to rekindle their romance.

At noon, Ellie closed down the shop for lunch. Business was always slow this time of year and she hadn't seen a customer for the past hour. So it was more than a little surprising when she heard the bells attached to the store's front door. Maybe the day wouldn't be a total loss after all.

But Ellie's surprise turned into shock and terror seconds later when she saw who—or *what*—had just walked in: a tall man with silvery skin who appeared human, but not quite human. There had to be a logical explanation for the man's appearance, she thought to herself in a futile effort to dampen her growing panic. An actor in some alien invasion film shooting nearby, perhaps?

"Hello, Ellie," Cooper said. Ellie's face turned ashen—how did he know her name?

"Who . . . are you?" she struggled to say.

"An old friend."

Cooper moved toward her and she backed away into a corner behind the cash register next to a display of a dozen or so music boxes. He smiled and said, "Don't be afraid, Ellie. It's me."

Ellie's eyes darted around, looking for a way out. She reached into her coat pocket and pulled out her cell phone, but it flew out of her hand and smashed against a wall.

"Help!" Ellie tried to shout, but Cooper's eyes flashed and no sound came out of her mouth.

Cooper now gestured toward the middle of the store. His eyes flashed again and an image materialized. An image of a young Cooper Brooks and Ellie Fernell on one of their picnic outings from many years before. With equal parts fear and fascination, Ellie stared at the image, trying desperately to process what she was seeing.

"*Now* do you remember?" Cooper asked, his voice uncharacteristically sentimental.

"*Cooper*?" Ellie said shakily, her voice returned to normal.

"Two-point-oh."

"But how . . . I thought you were serving time. How did you get out?"

"I can do whatever I want now."

"My God—what did they do to you?"

"Made me better. A lot better."

"I don't understand."

"You don't have to."

Still huddled in a corner like a frightened child, Ellie suddenly started shaking.

"Oh, God. I know why you're here. I'm so sorry I hurt you, but I was just a kid."

Cooper smiled. "I'm not here to kill you, Ellie. I don't hate you. I love you. And I want us to be together again."

Cooper's eyes flashed again, and all at once, all twelve of the music boxes on the shelf next to Ellie started playing simultaneously—a bizarre cacophony of melodies that turned her charming frontier gift shop into a nightmarish house of horrors.

"Help!" Ellie shouted. This time Cooper let her scream at full volume because it couldn't possibly be heard over the sound of the music boxes. But a moment later, he focused and the music boxes, and Ellie herself, went silent.

"I'm starting to lose my patience," Cooper said, his voice now more ominous.

Wondering why she didn't think of it before, Ellie slowly sidled away from her corner and moved a bit closer to Cooper—praying he wouldn't notice her pushing a button below the counter that would alert the police. Protection her father had insisted on when she opened the shop five years ago.

"Forget this store and forget this town, Ellie," Cooper said. "I can give you anything you want in the world. Think of me as the gift that keeps on giving."

His eyes flashed and gift items from throughout the store started to float toward the stunned Ellie. In a matter of seconds, the counter in front of her was a foot deep in assorted items running the gamut from scarves to monogrammed pillows to boxes of chocolate to bracelets, earrings, and necklaces.

"What do you say, Ellie? Pick up where we left off?"

Before Ellie could answer, they heard the sound of police sirens. Cooper looked over at Ellie with equal parts fury and despair. For a moment, he considered bringing the store crashing down on top of her or sending the two approaching police cars flying off into the side of a mountain, but he wanted to lie low outside of Caribou Bay for now—his visits with Zeke and Ellie notwithstanding. After all, it was time to pay Mayor Orrin Parker a visit, and nothing could stand in the way of that. Nothing.

Cooper looked one last time at the trembling Ellie and said, "Your loss." As four armed cops burst in the front door, he vanished out of the back and broke into a fifty-mile-an-hour run headed directly toward Main Street in Caribou Bay.

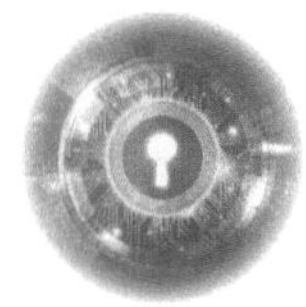

CHAPTER THIRTY-TWO

Cooper was standing midpoint between two poles supporting power lines. He focused his attention on the lines, his eyes flashed, and at once, the lines between the two poles started giving off a flurry of sparks.

A series of sparks hit Cooper and he reacted—surprised to feel pain. He directed his attention toward Mayor Parker's office building.

Inside the building, Orrin was at his desk, hanging up the phone as his secretary Diane looked on.

"Governor authorized a National Guard unit," Orrin said. "They're on the way."

"Won't be soon enough for me," a relieved Diane said.

As she left the room, Orrin became aware of a strange sound coming from outside—like paper crackling or a fuse box humming. Just then, the wall facing the street suddenly started cracking and shaking. Then it split in the middle, the two sides folding away from each other like two huge upright sections of aluminum foil being rolled in opposite directions. Pieces of the wall and the shattered glass of the windows came crashing down in the office.

From outside, a snake-like coil of thick wire writhing with blue electrical flame flew through the air and landed on Orrin's desk. The wire twisted and turned, sparking with deadly energy, scarring everything it touched. Orrin jumped up, barely missing the coil as a second coil slithered into the office, writhing and flying right toward him. It was quickly followed by yet a third coil, sputtering as it scorched the curtains and carpet.

Orrin hugged the wall, inching toward the door. Just outside his office, Diane and half a dozen people drawn to the commotion peered into the mayor's office, then retreated in terror. Only Diane remained.

"Help! Someone get help!" Diane shouted.

It was at this very moment that Tom, who had gone to Steiger's to load up on ammo, rushed up the stairs toward Orrin's office.

By now, Orrin was completely cornered, all three electrified coils dancing and writhing before him like trained snakes, waiting for the command to strike.

Cooper entered through the space where the wall once stood as Orrin stared incredulously.

"Judgment day, Your Honor," Cooper said. "The sentence is death by electrocution."

The coils edged closer, preparing to strike. Tom now rushed in past the terrified Diane and saw what was happening in Orrin's office. He hurried back into the corridor, broke a nearby emergency glass panel, and grabbed the fire ax within.

Inside the office, Orrin had contracted to a fetal position as one of the coils advanced beyond the others, dancing within inches of his body. Tom now rushed into the room, ax raised, and cut the lead coil in half. Like a severed snake, the half closest to Orrin continued to flail wildly for a moment, then went dead. The two other coils remained in position, floating in the air in front of the mayor.

"Cooper—no!" Tom shouted.

Now Tom quickly moved to the drawer in Orrin's desk and took out the new gold-handled gun and loaded in some extra clips. He raised the gun and looked at Cooper, hesitating—the hardest decision of his life. Then he fired a single shot that hit Cooper in the shoulder. The physical impact was minimal, but the emotional impact was incalculable—how could his own brother do such a thing?

Furious, Cooper returned his attention to Orrin, and the two remaining coils reared up and struck. In that same instant, Tom fired again, but it was too late for the mayor.

The unexpected force of the impacting bullet and reflex action sent Cooper backward, causing him to fall on top of the sizzling coils and react to the pain of contact. In seconds, the coils short-circuited his body. Tremendous convulsions wracked his frame, and then—at last—he was still and the coils fell to the ground.

Diane tentatively entered, then reacted to the sight of Orrin lying lifeless on the floor as Tom knelt beside him and shook his head. Then Tom moved toward Cooper in time to see a remarkable metamorphosis as his charred skin began to lighten, reconstitute, and return to its metallic tone. And then the bullet wounds began a similar transformation, healing in a matter of seconds.

"Oh, my God!" Diane said.

Tom dropped to one knee and whispered, "Cooper?" His brother's eyes were as deep and strange as space. The pupils glowed and faded, then glowed with life again. His expression reflected total bewilderment—he still couldn't believe what Tom had done. And then his eyes closed and he was unconscious. Diane inched a bit closer.

"Is he dead?" she asked.

"No. Get Charlie Porter. And find Dr. Lochman. Hurry!"

Happy to get out of there, Diane bolted off.

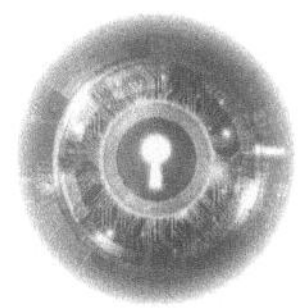

CHAPTER THIRTY-THREE

Fifteen minutes later, Mulroon's four-wheel drive raced up. Mulroon and Layton got out, then hurried into the building.

When they arrived at Orrin Parker's office, Tom was there along with Charlie Porter, two Kamcheka guards, and Dr. Gene Lochman.

Mayor Parker's body had been covered with a blanket and Lochman, looking more than a little dazed, was kneeling beside Cooper's unconscious figure. Layton, carrying a satchel of his own, noted Lochman's medical bag.

"How is he?" Layton asked.

"Alive," Lochman replied. "The real question is—*what* is he?"

Layton dropped beside Cooper and took out a large syringe, drawing fluid into it from a vial.

"My God, man—that's enough to tranquilize three elephants," Dr. Lochman said.

"Make it enough for the entire herd," Charlie Porter added.

"Be careful with him," Tom said as a perplexed Charlie looked his way. "He's my . . . brother."

Charlie's eyes opened wide, as did Lochman's.

"I want to get him back to Kamcheka—fast," said Layton.

"Who are you?" Lochman asked, but it was Tom who answered.

"Dr. Emory Layton, CEO of GenQuest Bio-Tech," Tom said bitterly. "The man who's responsible for all of this."

Layton's head dropped, then: "I'll answer all of your questions back in the lab, but we have to take him now."

"You know there's no way you can restrain him for long, don't you, Doctor?" Tom retorted.

"He's injured and the tranquilizers will keep him sedated for hours," Layton responded.

"And then what?"

"First things first, Mr. Brooks."

Tom looked down at Cooper, torn, then said, "I'll take him in the chopper."

"I'm here however I can help, Tom," Charlie said.

Tom patted her gratefully on the back and headed out.

Ninety minutes later, Tom and Layton were watching Cooper through the thick glass picture window that separated them from the processing area below. In the control room with them were two white-coated scientists and one technician.

In the processing area, a comatose Cooper, surrounded by several armed guards and medical personnel, was stretched out on an operating table. Thick titanium bands circled his body. Behind his head, a huge intravenous device pumped enormous amounts of a liquid tranquilizer into his arms and through his body.

Back in the control room, Layton turned to the others and said, "Gentlemen, excuse us, please."

The three men left. Tom remained at the picture window as Layton took a seat in front of a computer monitor.

"He's remarkable, you know," Layton said.

"He used to be my brother."

Tom stared at Cooper and then angrily asked, "What happened to him, Doctor?"

Layton beckoned and Tom settled alongside him to face a computer monitor. Layton hit the keyboard, then gestured toward the processing area.

"The process involves cellular acceleration through the use of a new type of kalopheen ray I developed. By radically accelerating the chromosomal structure, we hoped to create a powerful new human antibody to combat disease. I had tested a much milder mixture on a young lady with terminal cervical cancer and almost immediately, she was in remission—quite possibly permanently."

"But that wasn't good enough for you, right?"

"It seemed only logical that a more powerful dose could help ward off other diseases as well—perhaps one day *all* of them!"

"What went wrong?"

"Your brother's response was especially promising—enough to warrant a second kalopheen processing. The effect was a complete genetic restructuring, almost the creation of a new species."

"What are you trying to tell me, Doctor?" asked Tom with an edge.

"Somehow . . ." Layton said with awe in his voice, "your brother has evolved, I would guess, at least 250,000 years into the future."

Tom stared at Layton in shock.

Now Layton punched some keys and directed Tom's attention to the monitor as a computer-generated pre-historic man morphed into contemporary man and then into the man of the future—a figure resembling the transformed Cooper.

"Are you saying . . . that's what we're all going to be like one day?"

"To some extent, yes. But his evolutionary restruc-turing was artificially induced in an extremely compressed period of time. For that reason, it's impossible to know whether he represents a predetermined future or only one possible outcome. What I do know is that your brother is 2,500 centuries ahead of present-day man. And if I'm right, he uses at least 75 percent of his brain while we use about 10 percent."

"Still—all that power . . . There's got to be some-thing else fueling it."

"You're quite perceptive, Mr. Brooks. I can't be sure this explains it, but his processing also involved an experimental form of gamma radiation. In combi-nation with kalopheen, I believe he was essentially . . ."

"Given the powers of a god."

"Well, yes."

"Let me get this straight," Tom said with barely contained fury. "All this time, you've known you created a monster who's been killing innocent people, and you did nothing to stop him?"

"Not so, Mr. Brooks. We didn't know about the killings until very recently and we've done everything possible to track him down since he escaped."

"Bullshit, Doctor Layton! You and Mulroon knew who he was, but you didn't tell his own brother? Didn't it occur to you that he might contact me?"

"Yes, of course. Which is why we've had guards stationed at your house and your friend Claudia's condominium for days."

"How thoughtful. Then you must have known my ten-year-old son just came to Caribou Bay for the summer. Meaning you put him and my fiancée—not to mention the entire town—in grave danger. And the worst part is, you let me and everyone else believe that . . . hologram . . . was real and that my brother was fine and dandy in his cell when you should have been calling in the Army, Navy, Air Force, and National Guard from day one!"

"As I told you, we didn't know the extent of his—"

"No, Doctor—you didn't *want* to know. You didn't want to undermine your hush-hush program or jeopardize your government funding."

"You've got it all wrong, Mr. Brooks. I'm a doctor. My life is devoted to helping others. And I'll carry the guilt of what has happened with me the rest of my life. But it was never about the money. It was about the possibility of wiping deadly diseases like cancer off the face of the earth forever. It was about saving lives, not taking them."

"At what price, Doctor Layton?"

The two men remained silent for a moment, then Layton asked, "What was he like?"

The question was almost conversational—and so unexpected that Tom looked over uncertainly.

"What do you mean?"

"As your brother."

"He always had a short fuse, even as a kid. Always trying to prove something. And then our parents died when he was just a boy and it all turned to rage. Nothing was ever right again. On the run, in and out of jail, petty crimes, then harder stuff. Finally, he seemed better and I got him a job at a local hardware store and he was okay for a while. But the yard manager kept pushing him around, and one day, Cooper lost it—bashed the guy's head in with a shovel. Owner saw the whole thing. Cooper got fifteen years from the judge. And then he got 250,000 years from you."

Layton looked off pensively.

"What is it?" Tom said.

"He's still evolving. Perhaps as much as one thousand years every twenty-four hours."

Layton pointed to a series of graphs and other data on the monitor, all depicting every change in Cooper's body, a bewildering digital assault.

"Even unconscious, his strength may be growing," Layton said.

"But that doesn't worry you, right?" Tom asked sarcastically. "Because he's 'tranquilized.'"

"The computer recalibrates the dosage every thirty seconds."

"He grew an arm back, Doctor. His bullet wounds healed like crazy glue. You trust a computer to keep up with that?"

"I do," Layton responded stubbornly.

"Okay, everything's under control. You've got this advanced piece of meat on a metal slab and you're running some kind of super-strength tranquilizer through him with a garden hose. Then what?"

"Study him! Learn everything we can from him."

"While he lies there like some circus attraction. You planning on selling tickets, Doctor?"

"What choice is there but confinement?"

"What kind of life is that for him? The question is—can the process be reversed?"

Layton paused a moment, then tentatively said, "No."

"I don't believe you!"

"He's a miracle, Mr. Brooks. He might be able to save humanity a quarter of a million years of painful, slow, and deadly evolution."

"Isn't all this what Darwin would call *unnatural* selection, Doctor Layton? Evolution is *supposed* to take time—that's kind of the whole point, right? Then you come along and give it a giant kick in the ass and call it a miracle. You know what—I call it a nightmare."

"Of course the process will be modified next time, Mr. Brooks. And of course we can't have average people running around with virtually limitless telekinetic power. But my mistake wasn't in trying to speed up evolution, it was in choosing someone like your brother as a volunteer. A convicted killer who would, by his very nature, want to use such power to do harm."

"Do you hear yourself, Doctor? 'Next time'? There won't be a next time. It's over."

Tom stood up, deliberately hoping to physically intimidate the older Layton.

"I'll ask you again—can it be reversed?"

After a long pause, Layton finally nodded. "There may be a way. I need to contact a colleague in Japan."

"Then what are you waiting for?"

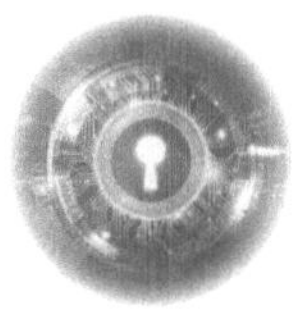

CHAPTER THIRTY-FOUR

NOVOSIBIRSK, RUSSIA

The young man tremulously entered the vast lab and spotted Dr. Sergei Baranov—stern and imposing as always—at a console. He approached his boss gingerly, knowing the doctor hated to be interrupted and had a hair-trigger temper.

The young man stood next to the seated Baranov for a full minute, too afraid to say a word. Finally, the doctor became aware of the younger man's presence and shouted in Russian, "What is it!"

His hands shaking, the young man produced a tablet, and in a quivering voice said, "Encrypted message just in, Doctor."

"From?"

"Our contact at GenQuest Bio-Tech. In Alaska."

"I know he's in Alaska!" But Baranov's demeanor suddenly softened a bit after he took the tablet and began reading the message, which was in English:

Exceptional news! Our subject has been captured and returned to our satellite facility at Kamcheka Point Federal Prison (location and schematics attached). I have tapped into our diagnostic mainframe there and have also attached all the latest readouts for your review. As mentioned in my previous messages, his abilities grow exponentially by the day—even by the hour—and I wonder how long it will be before he again escapes the prison lab.

If you are able to extract him from there in the very near future and study him in person, I am more confident than ever that you can accelerate your program by years if not decades and emerge with a replicable formula that will render your military utterly invincible and, frankly, render your current efforts unnecessary and obsolete.

Finally, let me once again respectfully warn you that although he is restrained for the moment,

our subject has powers beyond anything known in human history. Please make certain you are prepared for any and every eventuality.
Y

Baranov handed the tablet back to the young man and did the most unexpected thing imaginable—he smiled.

"Good work, Alexei!" Baranov said to the stunned young man.

"Thank you, Doctor," Alexei said, more than happy to accept Baranov's gratitude despite having done nothing more than delivered a message. *Thank God it was good news,* he thought as he walked off triumphantly.

What Alexei couldn't possibly know is that Layton had given Baranov and all of Russia a gift of unimaginable importance. Somehow, the American doctor's erroneous calculations and misguided formulations had turned an insignificant loser named Cooper Brooks into the most advanced being the world had ever seen. If his informant's reports were accurate and if the data he had sent continued to check out, Cooper had actually somehow evolved centuries into humanity's future in a matter of days.

And if Cooper Brooks could be studied and the process that altered his genetic makeup could be replicated, Russia itself would instantly evolve so far ahead of the rest of the world that no nation could ever possibly catch up.

Cooper Brooks didn't know it, but he was about to defect to the Motherland.

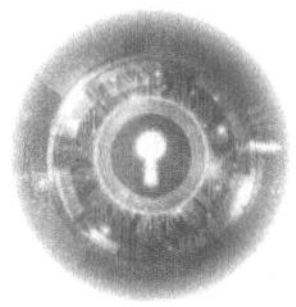

CHAPTER THIRTY-FIVE

As they headed to the doctor's private office to make the call to Japan, Layton briefly filled Tom in on a few salient facts. Prime among these was how a noted geneticist named Dr. Louis Garrett had first pioneered kalopheen-based genetic acceleration over a decade ago and how his process had later been misused to create the radical prison program called TimeLock.

Like most everyone in the country, Tom was familiar with TimeLock, given that for a while it was the law of the land in almost all fifty states. And like at least half the people in the country, he found it to be an abomination—a cruel way of dispensing punishment to convicted criminals by almost instantaneously aging them the number of years of their sentence.

Right now, however, what was of greatest interest to Tom was this—before TimeLock was approved by the government, Dr. Garrett had tested the process on himself to be sure of its efficacy. Unfortunately, instead of aging himself a couple of years, he had underestimated the true power of the kalopheen mix and had aged himself a full thirty years—from thirty-five to sixty-five. Happily, though, five years ago, Dr. Garrett had found a way to reverse the aging process and was today a healthy forty-year-old.

"And you think this same reversal might work on Cooper?" a hopeful Tom asked as he and Layton entered the private office.

"Only Dr. Garrett can tell us for sure."

Ten minutes later, Layton had just finished updating the Kyoto, Japan-based Louis Garrett on what had happened to Cooper and the seemingly boundless scope of his deadly powers. During the video call, Louis had asked his houseguest and brother-in-law Yoshi Ito to join in the conversation since he worked for Layton and might be able to help.

But after hearing about the swath of death and destruction Cooper had left behind in Caribou Bay, a tearful Yoshi looked into the camera toward Tom and said, "I'm so sorry . . ." over and over again.

"How is this your fault?" a confused Tom asked.

"Dr. Layton would never have fast-tracked his program if not for me."

"I don't understand," Tom said.

"My fiancée had months to live. That's why I was trying to reserve the banquet room at the Bayside Inn the night you and I met. So Katie and I could be married before I lost her forever. But Dr. Layton offered to test a new process on her. And it worked!"

"How is she, Yoshi?" Layton asked.

"In full remission. I think she's going to make it."

"Listen, Yoshi," Tom said. "I'm happy about your fiancée and I don't blame you for trying to help her, but we have more pressing issues to deal with right now. Dr. Garrett, can it be reversed?"

"This is uncharted territory, Mr. Brooks. But we can try. Emory—send me all the readouts on your . . . patient, and I'll see what I can do. I would come there myself, but there isn't time and my wife is about to go into labor."

"*I'll* come," Yoshi said. "It's the least I can do."

"I'm not sure that's necessary," Layton said. "I've got it under control."

Tom glared at him and Layton got the message. "On second thought, Yoshi, I could use all the help I can get."

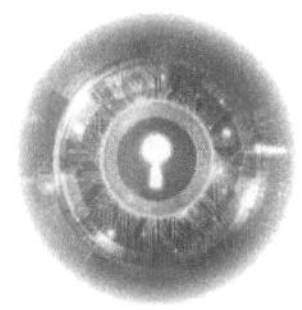

CHAPTER THIRTY-SIX

Despite Cooper staying sedated over the next few hours, Tom remained desperate to get Jordan and Claudia out of Caribou Bay. Unfortunately, a new storm had moved in and the bridge was still down, so transporting them to Juneau was out of the question for the time being. All Tom could do was ask Charlie Porter, Harry, and a few others to keep an eye on them.

A tense five hours passed before Layton finally received the data he had been waiting for from Dr. Garrett. With the help of his team, Layton quickly went about modifying the kalopheen mix and retooling one of the processing capsules.

Two long hours later, Cooper was placed inside the newly redesigned capsule, which then proceeded down the magnetic track as the kalopheen compound was sprayed within.

Ten minutes later, the capsule came to a stop and the glass top automatically opened. Tom and Layton hurriedly moved toward the capsule and waited anxiously for the thick spray to dissipate and clear the air. When it did, they exchanged elated looks—Cooper had returned to normal. No signs whatsoever of the metallic skin or silver hair.

The nightmare was over. Tom had his brother back.

"Coop?" Tom asked gently.

Cooper's eyes opened slowly and he let go a small smile.

"Tom? What are you doing here? I told them not to tell you."

Confused, Tom looked over to Layton, who said, "He means not to tell you that Cooper volunteered for our little scientific experiment." Then, in a whisper, he added, "He obviously doesn't remember anything that happened after he was first processed."

"Sorry, Coop," Tom said. "I happened to be visiting Jimmy Quine, one of the Kamcheka security guys, and he mentioned it."

"Doesn't matter. Well, Doc—how'd I do?"

"Beyond anything I could have imagined."

"Cool. Not that I have a clue what you did to me." Cooper smiled again before adding: "You know what this means, Tom. Early parole."

Tom forced a smile. Even if Cooper hadn't really known what he was doing, it was inconceivable that the powers that be would set him free anytime soon. Or ever.

Layton gestured to a couple of technicians, who helped Cooper out of the capsule.

"We'll get you cleaned up and then let you rest for a few hours, Cooper," Layton said.

An exhausted Cooper turned toward Tom and said, "See, big brother? I didn't let you down for once."

Tom squeezed Cooper's shoulder as his younger brother was gently escorted away.

"Well, Mr. Brooks," Layton said, "I'm happy for you and your family, but this is a great loss for medical science."

"Tell that to Teddy Newland, Orrin Parker, Leland Gaines, and Don Steiger."

A couple of hours later, Tom went to Cooper's recovery room. He pulled up a chair next to his brother, surprised to find he was groggy but still awake.

"Hey, big brother."

"Hi, Coop. How are you?"

"I don't know. I feel strange. What did they do to me?"

"Some kind of antibody stimulant," Tom said—making it up as he went along. "Supposed to help fight off diseases."

"And it worked? No side effects?"

Tom could barely answer, but managed a brief, "Guess not."

"They tell you when I might be paroled?"

"No. Not yet."

"Well, today's Friday. I guess I can wait till Monday."

Then Cooper checked his watch and noticed the date. "Wait a minute—this says June 7. Today's the fourth."

"No, Coop. It's the seventh. You've been . . . here for three days."

"Whoa. I don't remember any—"

His eyes opened wide.

"Wait a minute. That's strange—I just flashed on you and me at the beach."

"When we were growing up?"

"No—I mean, like it was just yesterday."

Tom wasn't sure how to play this. Triggering a flood of recent memories could jeopardize Cooper's recovery in untold ways. Then the obvious solution hit him.

"It's the drugs. Doctor Layton told me they can mess with your mind. Memory loss, hallucinations. Just focus on getting better."

Cooper hesitated for a second, then nodded. His eyes started to droop, exhaustion setting in.

"You need to rest, Coop. I'll see you in the morning," Tom said.

"Okay." But as Tom started to rise, Cooper gently touched his brother's arm.

"I'm sorry, bro."

"For what?"

"You kidding? I've been nothing but trouble since I was a teenager."

Tom smiled. "Well, at least we got twelve good years out of you."

"I'm serious, Tom."

Cooper paused for a full fifteen seconds, something obviously important on his mind.

Finally he spoke in an apologetic voice Tom never recalled hearing from his brother—a voice completely at odds with the terrifying basso profundo of the past three days.

"There's something you don't know. But if I tell you, you'll never forgive me."

"What are you talking about?"

It was the worst possible timing, but just now a team of nurses and technicians came in to check up on Cooper.

"We'll talk in the morning," he said as a curious Tom headed out.

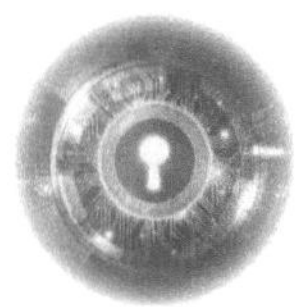

CHAPTER THIRTY-SEVEN

With a rough storm still raging outside, Tom decided to camp out at Kamcheka overnight. Truth be told, his real reason for staying was to make certain Cooper continued his recovery. And as much as Tom wanted to believe the horror of the past few days was over, neither Layton nor Garrett could guarantee that the reversal process would hold permanently.

At five thirty the next morning, Tom was still fast asleep on a sofa in one of the GenQuest Bio-Tech offices when he was jolted awake by the sound of gunfire. He bolted up and ran out of the office to find Layton and half a dozen technicians running from the recovery ward, past the processing area and into the control room.

"Hurry!" Layton yelled to Tom.

"What's going on?" Tom shouted.

"They're taking him! Your brother . . . they killed two guards and they're taking him!"

"*Who's* taking him?" Tom yelled but Layton was gone.

Just now, Mulroon and a dozen or so armed prison guards rushed in and moved toward the recovery ward.

"Warden—what is it?" Tom shouted.

"About fifteen guys with assault rifles. They landed in a pair of choppers and came straight here. I've got to go."

"Let me help. He's my brother."

Mulroon hesitated, then gave Tom one of his Glocks. Tom joined the others and ran toward the recovery ward. When they got there, they were greeted by a barrage of gunfire—three Kamcheka guards went down instantly. Peering inside the large space-age room, Tom could see several of the intruders carrying what he presumed was his brother on a stretcher toward a back exit.

Mulroon gestured and a group of his men raced down the hall to intercept the assailants taking Cooper out the back. Tom joined them as they reached a corner around which six black-clothed men were moving toward a rooftop exit door, Cooper still on the stretcher, apparently unconscious.

Several of the Kamcheka guards started to fire at the intruders even as Tom frantically urged them to stop for fear of hitting his brother. Indifferent to Cooper's fate, however, they continued to fire and hit two of the men as they attempted to flee.

Seconds later, the four remaining intruders carried Cooper out and by the time Tom and the guards got to the building exit, it was too late—their helicopter was already lifting off.

Tom and the Kamcheka guards entered the back door of the recovery ward, where a flurry of shots were fired on the cornered intruders, the last of whom collapsed dead on one of the ward's hospital beds.

Mulroon pulled out his cell and called for backup as Tom raced back to the building exit and out onto the helipad where one of the choppers had just taken off. He kept running until he spotted the intruders' other helicopter a few hundred feet away in a parking lot.

As Tom rushed toward it, gunfire exploded all around him. He ducked behind a van and spotted a pilot inside the helicopter, gun in hand. Tom circled behind several cars until he was just below the chopper, rotors whirling and waiting to lift off.

Just then, the pilot spotted Tom and fired at him. Tom raised his Glock and fired back, hitting the man in the shoulder. Tom climbed up and pulled the injured pilot out of the cabin, grabbed his gun, and knocked him out with a hard right.

Tom sat in the pilot's seat and realized he had never been in a craft like this. And no wonder—it was a Russian Mi-35M, primarily designed for military transport missions.

Tom scanned the instrument panel. "Here goes nothing," he said out loud before lifting the beast up into the air. Setting it down again would be another story, but he'd have to tackle that little problem later.

Despite the weather, Tom was able to spot the other chopper—the one carrying Cooper—fairly easily, so he thrust his helicopter forward at max speed and gave chase.

Tom was working on pure instinct now. The desire to protect his brother outweighed all logic since there was no way he could catch up with the first chopper and, more to the point, no way he could stop it if he did.

The only thing Tom could do now was visually follow the flight path of the first helicopter, which, in

this case, was due northwest. But in a matter of minutes, the storm was closing in on Tom's flight path, so
he reluctantly turned back.

CHAPTER THIRTY-EIGHT

It was two hours later and all the relevant authorities from the FBI on down had been alerted and were en route—weather permitting. Unfortunately, the one person who could shed light on what went down—the pilot in the chopper whom Tom had shot in the shoulder—had swallowed cyanide before he could be interrogated.

Between the Mi-35M and the AK-47s used by the assault team, however, it was obvious this was a Russian operation.

"The question is—how did they find out about Cooper?" Layton asked after he and Tom got back on a video call with Louis Garrett.

"The bigger question is how the entire world hasn't found out," Louis said.

To which Tom responded, "Small town. There weren't all that many witnesses. And then there's this irony—the videos that were posted were so far beyond belief that nobody believed them."

"Except for the Russians," Layton said.

"Unless someone there tipped them off," Louis said. "Told them what a valuable asset Cooper would be."

"Makes sense," Tom said. "Only problem is—what happens to my brother when they realize they came all this way for the ultimate solider and went home with a military school dropout?"

Both Louis and Layton went oddly silent for a few seconds.

"What?" said Tom.

"Keeping him . . . normal . . . like he is right now requires daily treatment for at least a month," said Louis. "Without it, he could be back where he was after he escaped."

"That's just great," Tom said bitterly. "Okay. Obviously we need to find out where they took him. The FBI and CIA are on it, but tracking a single chopper in bad weather in the middle of nowhere is going to take time and that's one thing we don't have."

Tom went to another computer and called up a map of Alaska and Russia.

Almost talking to himself, he said, "It's safe to assume they'd take him back to Russia. But it's much too far in a chopper, and a private jet would be too conspicuous. That leaves a boat. Maybe out of Wales."

"Right," said Layton. "The closest town on Russian soil is only fifty-five miles away."

"Naukun," offered Tom as Layton nodded. "Obviously, that would just be a stopgap location before the long trip to Moscow or wherever they're ultimately taking him. A place where they can check him out, make sure he stays restrained and sedated."

"All makes sense to me," said Louis. "But finding your brother is only half the battle."

"You're right, Doctor. This has to be a military rescue."

"Well—as it happens," said Louis, "one of my closest friends is a high-ranking FBI agent named Janine Eberly. Let me contact her and see what I can find out."

"Thanks, Doctor. We'll be standing by."

Tom and Layton ended the call. Tom got up but Layton remained seated, his head down.

"Thank you for not stating the obvious, Mr. Brooks."

"What's that?"

"That the seven men who died here today lost their lives because of me. Because I created a monster."

"I was angry as hell at you, Doctor Layton. I still am. But my brother was the main villain in this story—not you."

Layton smiled weakly. "That leaves the role of 'mad scientist,' then."

Tom also half smiled. "The part is yours."

CHAPTER THIRTY-NINE

Louis! How are you?" a sleepy Morgan Eberly said as he answered the 4:30 a.m. video call from his dear friend. Not wanting to wake up Janine or their two children, Jackson and Danielle, Morgan went into the living room of their suburban DC home and whispered, "You guys alright?"

"We're fine," Louis answered. "But TimeLock has just reared its ugly head again and it not only involves Emory Layton but Yoshi too."

"Are they okay? What happened?"

"Let's just say the TimeLock program has . . . evolved. And, once again, not in a good way."

"What's going on?" an equally sleepy Janine asked as she groggily entered the room.

"Sorry—I tried not to wake you," Morgan said to Janine.

She smiled and waved him off, her only concern being Louis and his family. "Louis, what is it?" Janine asked as she sat on the sofa next to Morgan and took in the distress on Louis's face.

For the next few minutes, Louis filled his friends in on the events in Caribou Bay and watched as their eyes opened wide in shock.

"Good Lord," Morgan said. "What TimeLock did to the two of us was bad enough, but this is a thousand times worse."

"More like 250,000 times worse," answered Louis. "That's how many years Emory estimates Cooper has evolved."

"My God," said Janine. "How can we help?"

"I'm afraid I've saved the best for last," said Louis. "Make that the worst. Cooper was taken by the Russians, and I have a feeling our old friend Sergei Baranov is on the welcoming committee. Morgan, you've said for years you suspected he survived that night in Siberia, and Janine, you've heard rumors from some of your pals at the CIA that he's still alive, so I'm afraid you were both probably right."

"But I thought you said this guy Cooper was back to normal—or at least his version of normal?" said Morgan. "Wouldn't that make him worthless to Baranov?"

"Unless we medicate him daily, he'll begin to evolve again. And if that happens and if Baranov is able to replicate the process, that means our most formidable enemy in the world will soon have an army of Coopers with virtually unlimited power."

"Charming," said Morgan, before adding, "I've got to help."

"Forget it," Janine said. "You've done enough for flag and country. You're a husband and a father now and your tour of duty is over."

"You're right," said Morgan in seeming compliance before adding, "You're right that I'm a husband and father now, which is exactly why I have to protect my family by stopping these maniacs in their tracks. Besides, I owe it to Mikhail to help bring down the man who murdered *his* father in that Siberian prison."

For what seemed like the millionth time, Morgan replayed the night of the raid in Siberia in his mind and how desperately he had tried to bring Baranov to justice. Instead, it now seemed more than likely that the doctor had indeed managed to escape and that Mikhail—now a thriving high school student living with Morgan's mother in Maryland—might soon learn that Baranov was not only still alive but had just become a greater threat to the world than ever before.

"Damn it, Morgan," Janine continued. "You're a cyber security consultant, not a superspy. Let the experts handle this."

"I have to agree with your lovely wife, Morgan. This is way above and beyond," Louis chimed in shyly.

"Guys," said Morgan with a smile, "you both know me well enough to realize your sound logic will never get in the way of my impetuous stupidity. I have to do this."

Morgan continued to smile, but Janine and Louis were having none of it. Nevertheless, they did both have to acknowledge one inescapable fact—once Morgan Eberly set his mind on something, even something as foolhardy as returning to Russia to probably face a man who had almost killed him on his last visit there, nothing and no one could possibly stop him.

After a thoughtful moment, Janine finally produced a slight surrender of a smile and said, "Fine, but take the parka I bought you. Your old one makes you look fat."

"Yes, dear," Morgan said before leaning over, giving his annoyed but admiring wife a big hug, giving Louis a thumbs-up, rising, and heading back to bed.

CHAPTER FORTY

Tom, I'm scared. You've done your civic duty," Claudia said, unknowingly echoing the words Janine had just said to Morgan some 3,700 miles away in the nation's capital. The tears in Claudia's eyes were clearly visible on a video call, even with spotty reception.

"I have to see it through. He's family," said Tom, sitting on the same sofa at Kamcheka where he had spent the night.

"What next?"

"We bring Cooper home and you and I and Jordan live happily ever after."

"What do I tell him? You've been away most of the time he's been here."

"Tell him Harry and I had to go on a rescue mission up north because of the storms. And tell him I'll buy him a brand new iSphere750 tablet when I get back."

"You don't have to resort to bribery. Just come home safe. *I* could use a new tablet though," she said with a big smile.

"Tell you what—I'll buy one and you guys fight it out."

"Deal. I love you."

"I love you too."

Tom and Claudia disconnected just as Layton came in and gestured for Tom to follow. "Louis is calling."

They hurried off and went back to Layton's office.

"I spoke to Janine," Louis began, "and she'll do everything she can to expedite the FBI's response. But as you know, this is an international matter, so it's really out of their purview. She's coordinating with the CIA and Pentagon, but she also went to another source who still has tremendous influence in DC."

"Who's that?" Tom asked.

"Former President William Bartlett."

"Okay, I'm officially impressed," Tom responded.

"He reached out to the Department of Defense and they think they know who's behind this."

Louis then briefly filled Tom in on the raid in Siberia that took place five years earlier and the possible escape of Russian geneticist Sergei Baranov—the person most likely behind Cooper's abduction.

"Whether this was Baranov going rogue or a Moscow-sanctioned operation is anybody's guess at this point," Louis continued. "Either way, though, the bottom line is the same—if they can replicate what happened to Cooper among even a handful of Russian brigades, the entire world will be at their mercy."

Tom paused for a moment, then said, "Now that we know the why, we still need to figure out the *where*. Maybe Naukun to start, but after that . . . ?"

"Well, I have a thought about that," Louis said. "The very specific type of kalopheen Emory and I use is now in very short supply around the world."

"And I'm assuming you don't pick it up at your local pharmacy," said Tom.

"There are only five or six reliable suppliers."

"What about the black market?"

"I strongly doubt it," said Layton.

Added Louis, "Not much demand outside of a few researchers like Emory and me."

Then Layton again, "And much too volatile and dangerous for anyone to handle surreptitiously."

"Okay," said Tom. "Why don't you two look into recent deliveries on Russian soil?"

The two doctors nodded.

"That still leaves one gigantic logistical problem," Tom said.

"How to get your brother back," said Louis. "Well, I have some good news on that front as well. As soon as we can pinpoint Cooper's location, Bartlett will ask President Ayres to send an assault team to get him out."

"When you're ready to mount the assault, I'll go with you," Layton said. Then, reacting to the concerned looks on both Tom's and Louis's faces, he added, "I need to be there to manage Cooper's dosage or he'll revert back and then God knows what'll happen."

"You're forgetting something, Emory," Louis said. "Yoshi is on his way. He'll be landing in Juneau in an hour."

"You know I have the highest possible regard for Yoshi, but he's not a doctor and I have thirty-five more years of experience in this field than he does."

"Which means you're thirty-five years older, Emory. I was your age, remember?" said Louis.

"He's right," Tom said. "I'm sorry, but this is a job for someone younger. Let Yoshi handle this phase, then you take over as soon as we're back."

"Fine," Layton conceded. "On one condition."

"What's that?" Tom asked.

"You take me on a free tour of Mendenhall in your helicopter when this is all over."

"Let's compromise," Tom said with a forced smile. "How about I give you the senior discount?"

CHAPTER FORTY-ONE

One hour later, Louis discovered that a company called Wentech Genetisk Industries out of Sweden had been supplying a Novosibirsk, Russia-based firm called Advanced Genetics Collaborative with a highly reactive form of kalopheen for five years. Given that this was the exact formula both Louis and Layton had been using of late, plus the rumors that Sergei Baranov had been seen multiple times in this very same Siberian city since the Special Forces raid five years earlier, it was clear the pieces were coming together.

And then Louis uncovered the capper—Wentech had just shipped a rushed order to Advanced Genetics's new "ancillary laboratory" in Naukun, Russia—located a mere fifty-five miles away from Wales, Alaska.

Shortly thereafter—and in great part thanks to an authoritative push by Janine Eberly at the FBI in Washington—satellite images pinpointed the remote part of the already remote village of Naukun where Baranov and his team had apparently built a makeshift new structure. A structure hastily constructed, no doubt, to evaluate Cooper before the long flight to Novosibirsk.

With a destination for the US rescue operation now determined, Tom hurried off to Juneau and boarded a waiting military transport plane bound for Nome—about a three-hour flight. With him, he brought the medical equipment and barium-3 doses which Yoshi—himself on the way to Nome in a commercial plane—would need to maintain Cooper's shaky status quo.

After landing in Nome, Tom met up with the fifteen-strong special ops team assigned to the rescue. They picked up the waiting Yoshi, who introduced them to a good-looking man just over six feet tall who seemed to be in his early thirties.

"Hi, I'm Morgan Eberly," he said as he shook hands with Tom, and a beaming Yoshi looked on with gratitude that his dearest friend had decided to join them.

"Good to meet you," said a puzzled Tom.

"You're wondering who in the world I am and what I'm doing here," said Morgan with a warm smile.

"Eberly . . . Dr. Garrett mentioned the name. Your wife is CIA, right?"

"Well, right idea but wrong initials," responded Morgan. "FBI, actually. Since this is an international operation, it's out of her purview—though she's crossed that line before in Siberia."

"Morgan and Janine helped bring down Baranov in Russia five years ago," Yoshi said proudly.

"Well, his operation at least," Morgan chimed in. "Unfortunately, now we suspect Baranov himself got away. And despite Janine's very vocal objections, I'm here to do whatever I can to finish the job."

"Awfully brave of you, Morgan," Tom said.

"Or should that be awfully stupid of me?"

To which Tom replied, "I have to do this, but you can still back out."

Morgan put his arm around Yoshi's shoulder, smiled, and said, "And let this guy get all the credit? Let's go."

Tom, Morgan, Yoshi, and the others boarded two helicopters to make the forty-five-minute flight to Wales. Once they arrived, the group split up—five men, including one pilot, assigned to each of the two choppers.

Though Tom was an exceptional pilot, he wasn't in the military and he knew these guys were the best of the best, so he had no problem being relegated to passenger status during the operation. And while Tom's civilian presence would normally spark resentment, his piloting creds—not to mention his relationship to the target—made him a welcome addition to the team.

"Please let me again apologize," a nervous Yoshi shouted to Tom in the belly of one of the MH-60 stealth helicopters.

"What Layton did, he did on his own. You have to stop blaming yourself."

"Yosh, he's right," said Morgan. "This isn't the first time something to do with TimeLock has gone astray. Let's just make sure this is the last time."

"Thanks, guys," a reassured Yoshi said before turning to Morgan. "I have to ask—did Janine try to stop you from coming?"

"Only every hour on the hour for the last three days. But she realizes I'm just as stubborn as she is. And, most of all, she realized I owe it to Mikhail."

"You're a good man, Morgan," said Yoshi.

"Tell that to my wife," Morgan said with a smile. Yoshi smiled back but the sentiment was short-lived and his expression gave way to fear as the chopper made a sudden rapid descent and landed in Wales.

Tom took in Yoshi's ashen expression and said, "You okay there, buddy?"

"Never been on a helicopter before, actually. I was okay with the up, but not so much with the down."

Just then, the pilot announced that the entire rescue team—under the direction of Colonel Gary Montgomery—would assemble shortly to run down the operation before taking off for Naukun at two a.m.

Only three short hours from now.

CHAPTER FORTY-TWO

At 3:23 a.m., the rescue team's two helicopters descended on the small village of Naukun, Russia—relieved, of course, there were no signs as yet that their arrival had been detected by Baranov and his team.

As it turned out, Baranov's group had built a relatively small facility just a few hundred yards from the coast. Satellite images revealed that his team numbered about twenty-five, but at least seven of them were medical and technical experts, not military.

And because the facility was intended only for short-term use before Cooper could be safely transported to Novosibirsk—some 3,200 miles from Naukun—the building itself wasn't likely to be well fortified.

With Montgomery leading the way, the rescue team edged toward the facility at 3:40 a.m., everyone—including Tom, Morgan, and a stoic Yoshi—armed with M4 carbines. Five Russian guards were stationed outside the main entrance and they were easily taken down.

But as the rescue team moved inside, an alarm went off and chaos immediately ensued. Gunfire rang out from all corners of the building as guards emerged from what appeared to be a main room as well as from three side rooms used for housing and storage.

"Spread out!" Montgomery shouted. As the American team dispersed into secure positions behind heavy equipment, a half dozen guards raced in. Within seconds, all six were eliminated, though the American team suffered two casualties during the melee.

The gun battle continued for another five tense minutes as two more Russian guards were gunned down and several others hung back in apparent retreat. With the situation contained, at least for the moment, Montgomery turned toward Tom and said, "Go find him." With which Tom, Morgan, Yoshi, and three of the special ops guys ran into the main room, where they immediately spotted a seemingly unconscious Cooper strapped to a medical bed with a staggering array of tubes and wires sticking out of him. Two men guarding him were rapidly dispensed with, prompting three Russian medical personnel to go running frantically out of harm's way.

With the American forces giving them cover, Tom, Morgan, and Yoshi moved toward Cooper and began detaching the various tubes and wires attached to him. Yoshi took out a medical kit from his backpack and stuck a syringe in Cooper's arm.

Off Tom's questioning look, Yoshi said, "Just pray this works. If so, he should wake up soon and continue the reversal process."

Even as Yoshi finished the sentence, Cooper's eyes opened, and he quietly whispered, "Tom . . ."

Now Tom, Morgan, and Yoshi, protected by three members of the rescue team, guided a dazed Cooper out a back door that led to the outside. Then, just as one of the special ops men was yelling into his headset, "We got him!" he and his two colleagues were gunned down.

"Put your weapon down now and stop right there," a deep voice shouted. Tom dropped his gun as he, Morgan, Yoshi, and Cooper all froze in place and turned to find a tall, chiseled, and decidedly commanding man in his late forties approaching—machine gun in hand.

"Dr. Baranov, I presume?" Tom said.

"Still killing and torturing—what he does best," said Morgan.

A wave of recognition suddenly crossed Baranov's face. "Eberly? Is that you? You're . . . young again. So Garvey did find a way! I'll be damned."

"You already are, you sick fuck," said Morgan.

"Well, this is an unexpected bonus, I must say. I've been hoping to pay you back for Siberia all this time, and now you conveniently show up at my doorstep."

Baranov turned to Tom and said, "Do I know you?"

"No—but you know my family."

Tom looked over at Cooper, who was leaning on Yoshi and barely conscious.

"Of course—you're the brother. You must be very proud."

"Screw you."

"Sorry to make you come all this way for nothing, but we've decided to adopt Cooper into *our* family."

"Can't you see—we've reversed the process," said Tom. "He's no use to you anymore. And, in any condition, he would never work for you or for Russia."

"We know his reversal is temporary, Mr. Brooks. Then we study him and create an army of soldiers just like him."

"And what happens when you can't control your little band of super soldiers, Doctor? What happens when they have so much power they don't need you anymore?"

"Well, one thing is for certain, Tom," said Baranov. "You and your brother will be long gone by then."

Baranov faced Yoshi and gestured toward Cooper. "Let him go."

Yoshi hesitated. Just then, two members of the American rescue team burst in and started to fire at Baranov, but he casually turned and mowed them down in a matter of seconds.

"I said—let him go," Baranov repeated.

Yoshi looked over at Tom and Morgan pleadingly, but remained frozen in place, holding up the weakened Cooper. Baranov considered firing a bullet into Yoshi's head but hesitated, afraid of hitting Cooper instead.

"Maybe this will convince you," Baranov said as he took out a handgun, walked up to Morgan and put the gun to his head.

"Do you really want me to count to three?" Baranov said with a sadistic smile as he started to pull the trigger.

Suddenly, the wall behind Baranov began to crumble, pieces of cement and plaster crashing all around him.

Though almost crushed by the falling debris, Baranov managed to point his gun at Yoshi, but just as he fired, Morgan slammed into Baranov, causing the bullet to miss hitting Yoshi in the head by mere inches.

With Baranov's fate unknown but his guards fast approaching, Tom gestured to Morgan and Yoshi— time to get out of here. He then approached Cooper, startled to see his eyes flashing ever so slightly. Tom looked back at the collapsed wall and realized it could only have been his brother. Cooper had just saved their lives, but quite likely doomed his own.

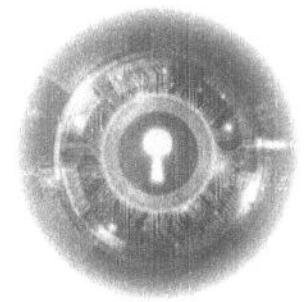

CHAPTER FORTY-THREE

Led by Colonel Montgomery, eight members of the rescue team made it out of the facility and ran toward the two waiting choppers. Tom, Morgan, Yoshi, and Cooper were the last to board, but as they climbed in, gunfire erupted from behind them, and two men were hit, including one of the pilots.

As Baranov and at least half a dozen men rushed toward them, Tom—assuming control of one of the helicopters after the loss of its pilot—and Montgomery fired up the two choppers and took off, heading out over the Bering Strait toward Alaska.

With dawn breaking on what at this time of year would be a nineteen-hour day, the two helicopters sped over the choppy water toward US airspace. Just then, though, one of two pursuing copters fired several missiles—one of which exploded only a few hundred yards from Montgomery's helicopter.

The craft sputtered and spun and Tom feared it would crash into the sea, but Montgomery managed to bring it down just past the international border on Little Diomede Island, Alaskan territory that was located a mere 2.4 miles from its Russian-controlled counterpart, Big Diomede Island.

"You're on your own, Tom," Montgomery said through his headset. "I'll call in for reinforcements."

"Thank you, Colonel. For everything," Tom said.

"Tom, watch out!" Morgan yelled as one of the Russian helicopters was closing in on their right side. And then the other chopper, with Baranov in the passenger seat, moved into a similar position on their left side. Tom reasoned they wouldn't fire on them for fear of killing Cooper, who was lying next to Yoshi and apparently still unconscious. On the other hand, they'd do whatever was necessary to prevent the Americans from getting their hands on him again.

As if reading Tom's mind—which Tom soon realized was exactly what had happened—Cooper suddenly sat up straight and looked out toward the water below. He concentrated intently and then his eyes flashed.

As if he were Moses himself, Cooper summoned the water beneath to rise hundreds of feet in the air and smash into the bottom of the two Russian helicopters. The one on Tom's right was overwhelmed by the freakish tsunami and spiraled down into the sea. On Tom's left, Baranov's pilot managed to veer away from the swell of water just in time to avoid contact.

"Don't worry, they won't fire on us," Tom said to a shaken Yoshi. "They want Cooper alive."

Just then, however, Baranov gestured and the men inside his chopper started to fire on Tom's helicopter.

"But I could be wrong, of course . . ."

"Don't worry, big brother," Cooper said. "I've got this."

Cooper's eyes flashed, and in a matter of seconds, the rotor blades on top of Baranov's helicopter broke free and hovered in the air as Baranov and his men looked on wide-eyed with terror. Expecting the chopper to fall, they were stunned to find that it, too, simply remained frozen in place—aloft only through the sheer power of Cooper's unbelievably advanced mind.

"Remember how much we loved boomerangs when we were kids?" Cooper asked. "I feel like playing now."

"Cooper—no! I want to bring Baranov back alive."

"No can do, Tommy boy," Cooper said, his features growing more metallic and his hair more silver by the second.

Cooper focused again, and Tom, Morgan, and Yoshi could only watch in amazement as the rotor system from Baranov's helicopter went flying out into space at a vertical angle. Moments later—just like a multi-pronged boomerang—the rotors spun around, soared back, and smashed into the front of Baranov's chopper. The craft broke into a dozen pieces that fell into the churning sea below.

A self-satisfied look crossed Cooper's face and Tom again realized he would never have his little brother back again. Tom gestured to Yoshi, who pulled out a syringe from his backpack and stuck it into Cooper's arm. An angry look crossed Cooper's face, but the dosage was too strong and he was out.

Less than five minutes later, the chopper started to vibrate and lose altitude.

"Shit!" said Tom.

"What's wrong?" Yoshi asked.

"Losing fuel. Must have been hit by gunfire back at Naukun." Tom looked over at Cooper. "We sure could use his help now."

"He's out for at least four hours."

"Swell."

"Can we make it?" asked Morgan.

"I hate to tell you this now, but I've never flown a military transport before. Putting it down in the water might be above my pay grade."

"In that case, I agree with what you said before," said Morgan.

"What's that?"

"Shit!"

Calling on everything he had ever learned as a chopper pilot over the years, Tom managed to keep the helicopter aloft, though barely. In fact, for a full nerve-wracking twenty-five minutes, he flew the chopper a mere thirty-five feet above the water—afraid of lifting her up and using up the small amount of fuel left.

Finally, the three men spotted land and Tom managed to bring the helicopter down on a rock-strewn beach a few miles outside of Wales, Alaska. They were exhausted, but they were alive, they were safe, and they were home.

CHAPTER FORTY-FOUR

Though relieved to have Tom and Yoshi back home safe, both Layton and Louis were obviously disappointed that Cooper's "remission" had proven so short-lived. And both agreed that trying the reversal process again would very likely prove fatal.

The Russian rescue ordeal behind them, Layton, Tom, and Yoshi were back in the Kamcheka control room overlooking the processing area where, as before, a highly restrained Cooper was lying unconscious. For his part, Morgan had headed back to DC and to a deeply relieved Janine after bidding a warm farewell to his old friend Yoshi and his new friend Tom Brooks.

Unbeknownst to Tom, Yoshi, and Layton, Cooper's eyes opened ever so briefly and he telepathically began tuning in to the conversation taking place among the three men in the control room.

"Where does that leave us, Doctor?" Tom asked.

"Back where we were before. We study him, we learn from him—"

"Let me rephrase my question—where does that leave *him*?"

After a long moment of silence, Layton said, "Mr. Brooks . . . Tom—I was trying to do something good, something important. And, God help me, I know he's still your brother."

"Used to be . . . 250,000 years ago."

"What are you saying, Tom?" Yoshi asked.

"Cooper is lost forever, and that . . . thing in there would be better off dead."

Hearing this, Cooper's eyes flashed and all the restraining bands flew apart. He jackknifed up, then turned to the nearest wall, which suddenly split open as though hit by an exploding shell.

In the same instant, armed guards and medical personnel in the processing area were swept off their feet and hurtled across the room, then sucked through the gap in the wall and out of sight with incredible speed.

Cooper started out as Tom, Layton, and Yoshi looked down through the picture window above. Before exiting, Cooper glared up toward Tom and suddenly the window shattered into pieces.

Tom turned to Layton and said, "Now what do you prescribe, Doctor?" As Layton and Yoshi looked on helplessly, Tom raced out, ran down a corridor and into a stairwell.

At this very moment, Cooper was inside a different stairwell, leaping up flights of stairs, then speeding past dozens of prison cells as the inmates within stared incredulously.

With the alarm now blaring and red lights flashing, Mulroon, joined by Tom, hurried into the prison armory where they picked up a rifle-mounted grenade launcher, along with a crate filled with grenades.

Outside the prison, tower guards broke out automatic weapons as they spotted Cooper running away from the compound and glancing back briefly with satisfaction. Before they could fire, however, the weapons were flung right out of their arms and sent hurtling to the ground below. Moments later, Cooper leapt over the tall prison wall, just as he had during his first escape days before.

CHAPTER FORTY-FIVE

Up on the prison helipad, Tom rushed out of the building carrying the grenade launcher, Mulroon right behind him with the box of grenades. Waiting for them with Tom's Bell 206 was Charlie Porter, who had gotten word from Tom a short while earlier.

As the weapons were loaded aboard the helicopter, Layton and Yoshi emerged from the building.

"I have to go with you. Please let me help," Layton said.

Tom reluctantly nodded, then looked over to Yoshi and Mulroon. "Sorry, guys. Too crowded already." Mulroon looked all too happy to be relegated to staying behind at the prison. Yoshi, on the other hand, wanted to continue helping however he could. Seeing Yoshi's earnest look, Tom gestured—hop on board—and Yoshi climbed into the chopper.

The Bell circled the complex before moving out in a wider arc. It then changed direction, cleared a ridge, and soared out over the surrounding mountains.

Inside the craft, Charlie, communicating with Tom and Yoshi through their headsets, said, "What're you thinking?"

"If we don't stop him, I've got to get Jordan and Claudia to Juneau."

Suddenly, Cooper's voice filled the cabin. "So I'd be better off dead, Tom? Not very brotherly of you."

Hearing Cooper's otherworldly basso profundo voice for the first time, Yoshi shook in stark terror and renewed guilt. He looked over at Layton and could barely get the words out: "My God—what have we done?"

But Layton ignored him and said, "Cooper—let us help you."

"You and my brother aren't making this easy," Cooper responded. "Let me see—door number one, I'm dead. Door number two, I spend my life as a guinea pig. Door number three, I rule the world. I think I know what door to pick. This one . . ."

The passenger door to Tom's chopper began to open.

"Doctor Layton," Cooper bellowed. "I don't think you appreciate the gravity of your situation."

Layton's seat belt unbuckled and a suctioning wind swirled around him. Tom tried desperately to keep the chopper steady as it bucked back and forth, bouncing around the sky and dropping hundreds of feet within seconds.

As Charlie and Yoshi desperately held on to Tom's seat belt, half of the front passenger seat was ripped away and sucked right out of the cabin, as was the grenade launcher Charlie had been holding. A split second later, Layton was yanked out of the cabin and began falling hundreds of feet to the rugged ground below.

"Oh, God," said Yoshi.

From the rocky hillside below, Cooper watched with amusement as Layton tumbled from the chopper. "Sorry, Doc. Your services are no longer required."

Back on the Bell, Charlie secured the door, and Tom finally managed to regain control. The copter began to climb as Tom, Charlie, and Yoshi—the latter two sitting on what was left of the passenger seat—reacted to the sound of Cooper's voice again filling the cabin.

"I wouldn't celebrate yet, Tom. And don't bet on you and the kid getting to Juneau. I've got other plans for our little family reunion."

Tom tugged on the controls and veered the chopper off in a sharp turn. He found a radio frequency, then fiddled with the radio, but it was dead. He then swerved the Bell toward Caribou Bay.

CHAPTER FORTY-SIX

Not far from Main Street in Caribou Bay—and, of course, *nothing* was far from Main Street in this small town—was the corporate headquarters of GenQuest Bio-Tech. Though Layton had spent most of his time at Kamcheka over recent weeks, this facility—part office, part research lab—was where Yoshi and the other twelve company employees normally worked.

Clueless about Cooper's metamorphosis and still uninformed about Dr. Layton's recent demise, the staff was hard at work when they felt a tremor in part of the building. Another Alaskan quake, no doubt. But this was different, they soon realized. The shaking was only happening inside one particular office! The office belonging to senior technician Victor Yullen.

As his horrified coworkers looked on, Yullen tried to run out of his office, but the door slammed shut and he was locked in. And now the group started to flee as Cooper strode onto the floor and moved toward Yullen's office. The door opened on its own and Cooper walked in to find Yullen huddled in terror in a corner. He looked to his colleagues for help, but by now they had all scattered out of the building.

"Hi there, Vic. I'm afraid I didn't make an appointment, so I hope you can squeeze me in."

"What—what do you want?"

"I think you know. You see, nothing escapes me. So when I was lying in a freezing room in a shithole building in the middle of nowhere with a thousand wires sticking into me as a guest of the late Dr. Sergei Baranov, I got to wondering. Did someone tell the Russians about me? I mean—they didn't just want me for my good looks, did they? And they had to know where to find me."

"I didn't . . ."

"Oh, but you did. Baranov told me all about it. Well, let's just say I picked up on his train of thought. And what he was thinking was that you had sold me out for $150,000. You should have held out for more. After all, I'm priceless, right?"

"I never meant . . ."

"Spare me. You found out what Layton was up to, you found out about me, you were kicked out of the Army, resented America, and wanted to ingratiate yourself with Mother Russia. Am I right?"

"I'm sorry . . . It was a mistake."

"Well, Vic—we all make those."

"Maybe I can help you. Tell me what I can do."

"Well, since Russia meant so much to you, I think you should prove you're willing to die for the cause."

As Yullen's eyes opened wide, a giant hammer and sickle suddenly flew into his office. They paused midair for a moment as a grinning Cooper looked on, and then began pounding and slashing Yullen until he fell, piece by piece, into a pile on the floor.

Cooper grabbed a handful of candies from Yullen's desk, then hurried off to his next meeting.

CHAPTER FORTY-SEVEN

A few blocks away at Tom's house, Jordan and Claudia were at work on the puzzle of Alaska. A little low-tech for Jordan, but he had to admit he was having fun. And he also had to admit that Claudia was kinda cool.

"Ready for my famous root beer sparkle-ade?" Jordan asked.

"You bet," said Claudia.

Jordan headed for the kitchen, but as he passed his bedroom, he heard a distinct humming sound. He eased toward the room as the door creaked open—first a crack, then all the way. And then Jordan's eyes widened in horror.

In the den, Claudia bolted up as Jordan let out a loud cry. She rushed toward his bedroom to find Jordan on his knees in front of his video game.

"The switch is stuck! It wiped out my record!" Claudia gasped in relief.

* * *

On the highway just outside of Caribou Bay, a fisherman and his wife in a beat-up pickup truck reacted as they spotted Cooper on a dirt road behind some shrubbery. Whooshing by them, he was doing at least fifty. Visible only from the shoulders up, the couple assumed the odd-looking man must be riding a motorcycle.

"He's crazy riding that thing off the main road that fast," the wife said.

The husband started honking at the "motorcyclist" and gestured for him to slow down.

Just now, Cooper emerged from behind the shrubbery and the pickup ran right off the road into a ditch as the couple saw he wasn't on a motorcycle at all. He was running!

Cooper waved to them as he sped off, but his look of satisfaction gave way to anger when he glanced up and became aware of two C-119 cargo masters zooming overhead, descending toward the Caribou Bay Airfield in the distance—both loaded with soldiers in full battle gear.

A few minutes later, Cooper watched as the first C-119 landed at the airfield. He focused on the plane, which then screeched to a stop and spun a full 180 degrees.

Inside the second plane, the pilot gaped through his windshield as he saw the other C-119 heading straight toward him. And then both planes crashed and erupted into a giant fireball.

Flying above, Tom and Charlie reacted to the ball of fire rising from the airstrip.

"Oh, Jesus . . ." Charlie said.

Now standing in a wooded area near the airfield, Cooper looked up and concentrated on the Bell 206, a sadistic smile crossing his face.

* * *

Jordan and Claudia were back working on the puzzle when the front door crashed in and splintered into pieces. "Come here, Jordo," Cooper said.

"Jordan—run!" shouted Claudia as she threw a table clock toward Cooper, which he easily deflected and sent crashing into the wall.

Jordan and Claudia tried to run but didn't get very far: the sofa suddenly slid across the floor and blocked their way and they both tumbled onto it.

"I said let's go," Cooper said to Jordan. He then looked at Claudia and ominously added, "It's okay—we're family."

Before Jordan could assimilate what he had just heard, he literally flew off the sofa to Cooper, who put him under one arm. Frantic, Claudia rose, but Cooper's eyes flashed and a heavy table slid across the room toward her. She jumped clear as the table slammed into the sofa, but then an armchair roared toward her and knocked her across the room. She bounced off the wall and fell in a heap, unconscious.

With Jordan squirming under his arm, Cooper paused before exiting the room. He looked over to the giant puzzle, still sprawled undone across the floor. The pieces began stirring, and, in a kaleidoscopic sweep, they started to join. With blinding speed, the pieces slapped together and seconds later, the puzzle was fully assembled—a full map of Alaska.

Cooper smiled at Jordan and said, "Looks like I don't need your help anymore." Noting Jordan's incredulous reaction, Cooper added, "That's right, kid. It's Uncle Cooper. Ready for some family fun?"

CHAPTER FORTY-EIGHT

A few moments later, Cooper and Jordan vanished into the forested area behind Tom's house, and a minute after that, Tom's helicopter settled on a nearby clearing.

Tom shut down the engines, then he, Yoshi, and Charlie jumped out. As they got closer, they spotted the smashed front door and raced into the house. Pushing furniture aside, Tom dropped beside the conscious, but still-dazed, Claudia.

"Baby, are you all right?"

Claudia blinked as Tom slowly came into focus. And suddenly, everything else did too, and she threw her arms around Tom and broke into tears.

"Oh, Tom, he took Jordan. I tried to stop him—"

Tom held her tightly. "Nobody could . . ."

He lifted her up.

"Stay with her," Tom said to Charlie and Yoshi. "I've got to find them." He moved toward the door as Charlie approached.

Charlie said, "What are you going to do?"

"I don't know. Anything I can to stop him. He's got my son."

"Then I'll go too," Charlie said.

"And so will I," Yoshi added.

"Not this time, guys."

"Where do you even start looking?" asked Charlie.

"Fishing cabin Harry built. Cooper was hiding there the night Teddy arrested him. Good place to start."

Tom hurried back to the Bell, climbed in, restarted the engines, and lifted off.

Back in the house, Yoshi approached Claudia. "You sure you're okay?"

"It's not me I'm worried about." She paused for a second, taking in Yoshi's sweet and deeply empathetic look. "I know you. I mean, I know who you are. Yoshi, isn't it? With GenQuest?"

"I'm afraid so."

Looking toward Charlie, Claudia said, "Help him, Charlie. He needs you more than I do. Take my truck. Yoshi can stay with me." She turned toward Yoshi and said, "If that's alright with you."

"It's the least I can do," Yoshi responded.

Claudia picked up her keys off the kitchen table and tossed them over to Charlie, who nodded and ran for the front door.

Half an hour later, the Bell was heading down toward the Juneau Icefield. Tom looked down and spotted the cabin among the trees within the forested area to his northeast.

He brought the chopper down between trees near the southwestern edge of the icefield. As the rotors came to a stop, he emerged from the helicopter and looked toward the forested area near the southeastern region of the icefield where the cabin was located.

Tom now pulled out Orrin Parker's gold-handled gun from his parka and started moving toward the cabin along the southern perimeter of the icefield.

Hugging the forested land at the edge of the icefield, Tom paused. Twenty- and thirty-foot-tall columns of glacial ice called seracs formed a stunning frozen skyline behind him, and off in the distance behind them was the entrance to an ice cave atop the icefield.

Tom cautiously approached the cabin, Orrin's gun at arm's length in front of him. He pushed inside to see a swath of light streaming in from a window and spilling across Jordan, who was seated in a rickety chair, awkwardly perched and terrified.

"Jordan!" Tom shouted, but Jordan didn't respond. Then Cooper emerged from the shadows. Tom spun and leveled the gun, but as he did it suddenly turned glowing white hot and Tom dropped it to the floor.

Tom took a close look at his brother. His face was now more metallic than ever and his silver hair had almost completely disappeared to reveal a pronounced forehead and slightly enlarged cranium.

"Right on schedule. Good old reliable Tom."

"Don't hurt him. I'm here. You've got what you want. Let him go."

Cooper turned to Jordan. "The thing is—your dad's not such a great guy. He wants me dead. His own brother. Now that isn't very nice, is it?"

"What happened to you?" a tremulous Jordan asked.

"I got better than dear old Dad. Maybe you'd be better off being *my* kid."

"Never . . . You're a monster."

Cooper's eyes flashed and a lamp went flying across the room and crashing into the wall. And then he turned to Tom and said ominously, "Maybe it's better this way. Out with the old blood, in with the new."

At this, Tom exploded with raw instinct. He rammed into Cooper, actually pushing him back against the wall. Cooper was briefly surprised by the fury of Tom's attack, the intensity of his emotion.

Then Cooper smiled, turning their confrontation into a game, like kids again, just horsing around. Tom was punching Cooper hard now, but his blows had no impact—other than to amuse Cooper. And then, Tom's anger and frustration gave way to a desperate pleading, and he ended up clutching his younger brother.

"Don't hurt him, Cooper . . . *please*," implored Tom.

Cooper seemed affected, but it was a pose: his eyes glowed and Tom was sent flying back across the room and against a wall. He fell into a heap and Jordan hurried to Tom's side.

"Dad!"

Tom's forehead was cut and bleeding. Jordan cradled his father in his arms and said, "I love you, Dad."

"I love you too," Tom said weakly.

"How touching," Cooper said. He turned to Tom and bitterly added, "You disgust me. You're worse than all the others. You were my brother!"

Cooper reached out and Jordan was instantly pulled into his hands. Effortlessly, he tucked the boy under his arm and moved to the open door.

Tom slowly rose as a taunting Cooper looked back and said, "Come on, Tom. You can do it. That's it. Tough it out, big brother. Wouldn't be any fun now without you."

Cooper now moved toward a clearing in the trees a hundred feet away, Jordan still under his arm. From there, the icefield was clearly visible less than a quarter mile ahead. Cooper turned back, smiling, as he saw Tom struggling to follow, slowly moving forward toward the clearing.

"Cooper—you're his uncle!" Tom yelled.

"Used to be," Cooper said in Tom's voice, "250,000 years ago."

Cooper looked toward the razor-sharp seracs of the icefield. Spotting him and Jordan some one hundred yards away was Charlie Porter—hidden behind an outcropping of rocks with a rifle in her hands.

Charlie fired and Cooper reflexively reacted to the unexpected force of the bullet slamming into his shoulder from behind. Then a second bullet slammed into his back, sending him forward to the ground. In this instant, Jordan broke free and ran toward Tom, even as the wounds on Cooper's back and shoulder started to heal.

Anticipating what was coming, Charlie quickly moved to another position just as Cooper turned toward the source of the bullets. His eyes flashed and several boulders crashed down on the spot Charlie had just abandoned.

His wounds now healed, Cooper focused on the fleeing Jordan and the boy was sent sailing through the air right back into Cooper's arms as a horrified Tom looked on. Now securely crouched behind another out-cropping of rocks, Charlie raised her rifle and pulled the trigger. This time, the bullet hit Cooper in the back of his head. He dropped to his knees, allowing Jordan time to again run toward a waiting Tom.

Cooper rose, but his balance was shaky—this wound was clearly more serious. He focused on the running Jordan and his eyes flashed, but less intensely than before. And this time, Jordan wasn't pulled toward him, but was instead able to continue running toward Tom.

Cooper put his hand on the back of his head and reacted to the sight of blood. He closed his eyes and concentrated, trying to heal the wound. After a few seconds, he took a deep breath and with it came renewed strength—he was still hurt, but he knew his powers remained formidable.

Cooper then started running toward Tom and Jordan—a bit stiffly at first, but then much faster. Then he spotted his quarry running along the edge of the icefield and paused, concentrating intently again, eyes flashing.

One by one, at least a dozen of the inverted cone-shape ice fragments were wrenched upward into the air like so many Excaliburs violently tugged free. They angled up, then aimed toward Tom and Jordan, crashing into a million particles all around them. They dove for cover as the missile-like seracs continued to crash near them.

"Jordan, run and hide!" Tom said, pointing toward the southeastern section of the icefield.

"Dad, I'm scared!"

"Do what I say—now!"

CHAPTER FORTY-NINE

Another serac speared its way toward them as Tom and Jordan ran to avoid it. Jordan headed off in the other direction, even as Cooper—still in pain but smiling sadistically—moved at a leisurely pace toward the edge of the icefield. As he got closer, he spotted Tom running off toward his chopper.

Tom reached the Bell nestled in the forest clearing, then climbed in and activated the engine and rotors. As he did so, Jordan continued running along the edge of the icefield before spotting an ice cave. He ran over the ruggedly solid icefield surface toward the cave's entrance.

For her part, Charlie was running toward the edge of the icefield, trying to get a fix on Cooper, Tom, and Jordan. She was holding the rifle but couldn't target

Cooper through the intervening forest area. Just then, she saw Tom's chopper rising above the forest.

At the same time, Jordan was approaching the cave when he saw Cooper headed toward him. Jordan rushed toward the cave entrance even as the Bell flew into the haze of the fog-covered icefield toward Cooper.

"Go, Tom, go!" Charlie cheered Tom on from below.

Still wobbly, Cooper was closing in on Jordan as he was running the final stretch toward the cave entrance. Cooper now became aware of the chopper approaching.

"Dad!" Jordan shouted euphorically. But then all hope vanished when the chopper materialized out of the haze and angled into a swooping dive—Tom was about to crash.

But inside the chopper, Tom was actually in complete control, his eyes fixed on his target: Cooper. Tom thrust a lever forward in a kamikaze run—anything to keep Cooper from Jordan.

Now Tom angled the Bell to its side, the path of the rotors now aiming toward Cooper's body. Cooper smiled and said, "This our game of chicken, Tom? I like mine well done."

Suddenly, the chopper was ringed by fire, just like the barbequed chickens that Cooper had cooked back in Caribou Bay. As Cooper headed toward the cave, Tom tugged at the controls, pulling the chopper out of its dive at the last possible instant with next to zero visibility and with flames dancing around the windshield.

The chopper staggered off in flames, its flight path erratic. It barely cleared the seracs, then disappeared out of sight as a stunned Jordan watched from just inside the ice cave.

No less aghast was Charlie as she, too, saw the chopper vanish above the icefield, the ring of fire still surrounding it. Cooper glanced over to see the flaming chopper disappear over the icefield, then returned his attention to Jordan. Now a new reality hit Jordan as he spotted Cooper moving toward the cave again. Jordan ran inside through a twisting passageway.

In the Bell, Tom was desperately fighting the controls, trying to see through the ring of flames and the mist. He struggled to make out an objective, then finally saw clearly enough to correct his direction.

Stabilizing, Tom flew over the forested area toward the waterfall—the very same one Frank Kaden had jumped into after being cornered by Tom and Charlie. Tom flew the chopper into the outer spray. Like a light, steady rain, it quickly put the fire out. Tom then flew back over the icefield, moving slowly, straight and level, toward the cave as a jubilant Charlie looked on. He then unfastened his safety harness and looked down at the instrument panel.

Just inside the mouth of the cave, Cooper paused in surprise as he heard the chopper. From his vantage point, the helicopter was again disappearing into the fog-like mist over the icefield. Cooper watched with amusement, waiting for the craft to reappear. Instead, he heard the sound of its rotors changing pitch, then powering up again.

Finally, the chopper emerged from the fog. It was still headed toward Cooper, but flying erratically, bucking up and down and barely staying on course.

With this, Cooper decided he'd had enough. His eyes gleamed and the copter's rotors came to a sudden, complete stop. The Bell plummeted down onto the seracs of the icefield just short of Cooper and the ice cave, smashing into the ice with metal-wrenching ferocity.

The sound of the crashing helicopter then set off a series of vibrations in the sheer wall of the ice cave. Small chunks of ice came crashing down. Cooper moved to the chopper, his curiosity too strong. He peered into the cabin. No sign of Tom. And then he spotted the autopilot switch flashing over and over.

Just out of Cooper's view, Tom—ducking between seracs—ran toward the cave entrance and looked over to where Cooper and the chopper were. Tom then slipped inside the cave entrance just as Cooper whirled and saw what was happening.

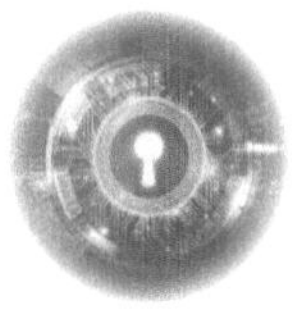

CHAPTER FIFTY

A true marvel of nature, the cave was constructed purely of ice formations with ice walls comprised of bizarre friezes twisted by time. The space was studded with enormous stalagmites and a forbidding array of stalactites high overhead, pointing toward the cave floor like an army of spears.

Jordan was in a corner, recoiling in fear, when Tom entered the chamber and spotted him.

"Dad!"

Tom ran to his son and they embraced. "Thank God you're alright. Now let's find a way out of here."

Now Tom noticed a corner of the chamber bathed in light. He and Jordan hurried toward it and saw that the light was coming from a fissure in a low-roofed section of the chamber.

But it wasn't low enough and Tom couldn't reach it. He then spotted several odd-shaped stumps of ice thrusting up from the surface and he and Jordan climbed on top. Tom picked Jordan up and was able to lift him to the fissure above and then push him up and out. Tom jumped up toward the open fissure, but his hands were too slippery on the ice.

"Going somewhere?" said Cooper, now entering the cave. "Game's over, Tom. Guess who won?"

But just then, a chunk of the ice wall came crashing down, striking Cooper and thrusting him to the ground. This allowed enough time for Tom—with Jordan's help—to lift himself up through the fissure.

Tom grabbed Jordan, and they slid wildly down across the icy dome that covered the cavernous ice chamber within. Clutched together, they slid onto the icefield at the base of the ice cave. Tom looked to Jordan, who nodded that he was alright.

Tom then grabbed Jordan's hand and tugged him toward the disabled chopper. A relieved Charlie came running toward them, gun in hand.

"Come on!" Tom shouted.

The trio raced to the chopper, then reacted as Cooper leapt from within the chamber floor to a perch on the cave roof. He spotted Tom, Jordan, and Charlie at the chopper and a bemused smile appeared on his face— they were trapped.

"Out of time, Tom."

"Alaska is the largest state in the Union," Tom said in an odd monotone. "Juneau, its capital, is known as the Gateway to the Glaciers."

Jordan and Charlie looked at each other—had Tom lost it?

"Alaska was officially proclaimed a state on January 3, 1959," Tom continued in the same emotionless flat tone as he reached into the cabin. Looking down, Cooper was no less perplexed, trying to tune into Tom's mind but unable to do so.

Tom turned on the emergency siren but nothing happened even as he continued the bizarre monologue he prayed was preventing Cooper from reading his thoughts. "Scientists estimate the Juneau Icefield's snow and ice depth to range from eight hundred to forty-five hundred feet," Tom continued, "with Mendenhall Glacier located just over twelve miles away."

More curious than annoyed, Cooper was still trying to reconcile Tom's actions with his tour-guide geographical babble.

Meanwhile, inside the cabin, the switch finally lit up. Tom pushed the button and turned the volume up to full blast, and a deafening siren blared across the entire area.

Within seconds, the tsunami of sound caused the cave walls to disintegrate in a thousand different places near and under Cooper's feet, with fragments of ice beginning to hurtle down to the chamber floor below. Suddenly, Cooper's section of the cave roof gave way, and he crashed into the cave chamber as its domed top continued to crack and fall down in widening sections. As soon as Cooper hit the bottom, a series of stalagmites started to plummet all around him.

One hit him right in the stomach and he closed his eyes in concentration. At last, he willed the huge icicle out—but not without wincing in pain. The gaping maw congealed, but the healing process took longer than it did before Cooper's head wound.

Barely recovered from his latest injury, Cooper now watched wide-eyed and helpless as a giant chunk of ice hurtled down and slammed into his chest. Another sword of ice struck him seconds later in the neck.

Above him, spiderweb cracks had developed and the entire roof was sagging and in danger of collapsing. But Cooper realized it no longer mattered—he was mortally wounded.

"Tom," he whispered. "Help me."

Though Tom was outside and the sirens were still blaring, he somehow heard his brother's cry for help. Against the vehement protests of both Jordan and Charlie, Tom shut off the sirens and then made his way into the cave chamber, somehow knowing Cooper's life was near its end.

Tom made his way to his brother's side and saw with a mixture of anguish and relief that Cooper was fading fast.

"Tom . . . You came back," Cooper said, his terrifyingly deep voice gone.

"I'm here. Let me help you. I'll take you to a hospital."

"No. The monster always dies in the end, remember? But first, there's something I want you to see."

Tom couldn't imagine what Cooper was talking about given the circumstances, but he nodded and watched as his brother summoned up what little strength he had left to perform one final "miracle."

"Remember I told you I did something . . . something you could never forgive me for?"

Tom nodded.

"Watch."

Ghostlike images appeared a few feet from where Cooper was lying. As they became clearer, Tom could instantly feel the tears welling in his eyes. He was looking at his father, Alex, and a young Cooper in the room he and Tom shared. Alex and Cooper were in the middle of a long hug.

"You were away at camp," Cooper said in a near whisper. "I had just accidentally shot a boy in the leg."

"Oh, my God," Tom responded, his voice quivering as he remembered his aunt telling him about the incident a few days later.

"Then this is . . ." Tom couldn't get the words out.

"The night Dad died. Because of me."

"I don't see how . . ."

"Keep watching."

After their hug, young Cooper said to his father, "I'm sorry, Dad. I'll try to be better. I promise."

"And I meant it, Tommy. I really did."

"I believe you," Alex said, the faint sound of thunder in the background. "We'll talk more when I get back."

"Don't leave, Dad . . . *please*!"

"I've got to get to the airstrip, Coop. You know I'm taking the Beechcraft up to Anchorage."

"Then leave in the morning."

"I can't. My flight to Boston is at seven in the morning. But I'll be back in four days."

The young Cooper looked on the verge of tears. But a new feeling was also clearly washing over him—anger.

"I hate to leave you like this," Alex said.

"Then don't!" Cooper snapped—mad at his father for leaving.

"I love you," Alex said as a wordless Cooper watched him leave.

"That's what this is about? That you didn't tell Dad you loved him? I'm sure he knew . . ." Tom told Cooper, whose breathing was growing more and more labored.

"You don't understand. Look."

Now the image changed to the young Cooper running out the front door and waving to his father as he climbed into his SUV. It was starting to rain now, but Alex got out and ran toward his son.

"I love you too, Dad."

They hugged again and Alex got in his car and drove off as Cooper went back in the house.

The images started to fade and a moment later, were completely gone.

"I still don't understand," a thoroughly perplexed Tom said. "You told him. That was the last thing he heard you say. Why would anyone blame you?"

"Don't you get it, Tom? If I had told him in our room, everything would be different. But I waited. I waited because I was angry at him for leaving again. I waited, and that's why he got to the airfield ten minutes later. If he had left when he was supposed to, his plane wouldn't have been hit by lightning and he'd be alive today!"

Now Cooper was crying and Tom found himself in the strange position of comforting someone who, minutes earlier, had been trying to kill him and his son. But that wasn't really Cooper, Tom reasoned. And for all the heartache he had caused over the years, this was his brother and he still loved him.

"Don't blame yourself, Coop. You did nothing wrong. You were just a kid. And the last thing Dad ever heard you say was 'I love you.'"

Cooper nodded weakly, his eyes growing dimmer, his pallor growing grayer.

"Thanks, big brother. So I guess it's time to quote Dad . . . 'I hate to leave you like this.'"

"Then don't," Tom said, his face blanketed with tears.

"I'm finished, Tom."

"No—that's not what I meant. I meant—don't leave me like . . . *this*."

Now Cooper understood. "I'm not sure if I can do it, but I'll try."

With Tom holding his hand, Cooper concentrated with the little bit of strength he had left. And slowly, the metamorphosis began and 250,000 plus years of evolution were again reversed until only Cooper Brooks—the *real* Cooper Brooks—was able to look his big brother in the eye for the very last time.

"I love you, Tom. Tell Jordan I'm sorry. Please forgive me."

"I love you too, Coop . . ." Tom said tearily. Seconds later, the roof of the cave began to collapse and Tom watched with despair as Cooper's body was blanketed in ice and snow. Tom rushed out of the cave entrance just before the entire structure collapsed on itself.

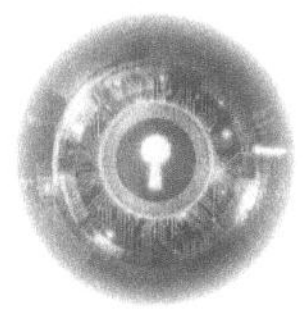

EPILOGUE

THREE MONTHS LATER

It took a while, but the residents of Caribou Bay were finally starting to put the horrors of the past summer behind them. And nowhere was the effort to move on better evidenced this warm September evening than at the picturesque Bayside Inn, where Yoshi and Katie were hosting their wedding party.

On hand this joyous night were Yoshi's sister Kiyoko, her husband Louis, and their two-and-a-half-month-old daughter, Aiya. Also happily celebrating the occasion were Yoshi's beloved pals from DC, Morgan and Janine Eberly, as well as their two children, Jackson and Danielle.

Among the other guests at the event were Yoshi's two new good friends, Tom Brooks and Claudia Hollister, who would themselves be married in this same venue three short weeks later.

Later that night, a reflective Morgan took Yoshi aside on a patio overlooking the bay and warmly said, "We have so much to be grateful for, don't we, Yosh? TimeLock has taken so much from so many, but it brought you, Kiyoko, and Louis into our lives and for that I'll be eternally grateful. And, my God, how we've all changed over the years. I went from being a young punk to a middle-aged fugitive to a young husband and father living a life I never could have imagined in my wildest dreams. And you went from being a shy, self-doubting young man to a hero who saved my life and so many other lives and who's just started a new future with an adoring and beautiful wife. Not bad for a couple of late bloomers, right?"

Yoshi nodded, but something was clearly on his mind. "I love that you can put a positive spin on just about anything. I really do," he responded. "But when I think what happened here—the people lost, a young boy traumatized, a peaceful town turned into a war zone . . . I still blame—"

Refusing to let Yoshi continue, Morgan interrupted and said, "You were trying to save the woman you love—and look at how that turned out." He directed Yoshi's attention to Katie, having the time of her life on the dance floor. "You promised to leave all that completely unwarranted guilt behind you, and I expect you to keep that promise. Okay?"

Yoshi finally produced a big smile and said, "Okay."

"Good, now get back to your beautiful bride before she wonders why she's dancing with her old father on her wedding night instead of with her young husband."

Yoshi gave Morgan a big hug, then went inside to celebrate with his new wife. A moment later, Janine, Kiyoko, and Louis joined Morgan on the patio.

"Everything good?" Janine asked.

"Perfect," a smiling Morgan responded, taking Janine in his arms.

"Louis—please tell me we've seen the last of TimeLock," Kiyoko said to her husband.

Louis thought for a moment before saying, "I hope so. God, I hope so. But all I know is that what happened in this town can never happen again."

"Hear! Hear!" said Kiyoko as she took a sip of champagne and the others followed suit.

"I think I remember it," continued Louis as Morgan, Janine, and Kiyoko looked on with curiosity. "'Learn from me, if not by my precepts, at least by my example, how dangerous is the acquirement of knowledge, and how much happier that man is who believes his native town to be his world, than he who aspires to become greater than his nature will allow.'"

"Louis, what's that from?" asked Janine in an almost reverent whisper.

"Mary Shelley wrote those words more than two hundred years ago in her novel, *Frankenstein*. And after what these people have been through, I can only pray that humanity evolves enough over the *next* two hundred years to heed those timeless words forever."

Three weeks later, on a mild Saturday afternoon, Tom and Claudia were in the garden at the Bayside Inn dancing closely, smiling and staring into each other's eyes. A couple dozen tables were set up on the lawn, all featuring elegant wedding decorations and floral arrangements. A small jazz band played from within a gazebo.

Charlie Porter and Diane Reid were among the others in attendance, as were Yoshi and Katie, who had recently returned from their honeymoon in Hawaii.

Beyond Jordan, Harry, and Dr. Gene Lochman, the celebrants included Tom's grouchy-as-ever Aunt Beth.

The dance ended and Charlie and Diane—quite possibly foreseeing many future evenings together—headed off to get a drink. Jordan approached Claudia and shyly extended his hand for the next dance as the music began. Tom smiled and walked over toward Charlie as Diane settled at a nearby table. He picked up two glasses of champagne and handed one to Charlie.

"Here's to our next chief of police," Tom said as they clinked glasses.

Charlie smiled. "One Indian chief joke and you're behind bars."

Tom laughed and then Charlie added, "You hear about Mulroon? He resigned."

"Made out better than Dr. Layton."

Though Layton had perished, the important work he had been doing at GenQuest before Cooper's transformation was continuing with Louis leading the team from his home base in Japan and Yoshi running day-to-day operations in Caribou Bay in his new capacity as company COO.

Meanwhile, Baranov's research facilities had been completely dismantled and the Russian government destroyed all evidence of what the late doctor had been undertaking. However, in light of America's own complicity in what had transpired given that Layton was a US citizen and GenQuest Bio-Tech was a DC-funded genetics company, the decision was made to let Russia's role in the whole affair remain buried forever. And since the events in Caribou Bay had miraculously never become public, the United States and Russia were able to agree on the only strategy that made sense for both sides if indeed word ever did get out: mutually assured denial.

Tom clinked Charlie's glass again and with a wan smile said, "Here's to Teddy. Best man forever."

They sipped from their glasses. Suddenly, they both turned to the sound of a helicopter approaching. Everyone looked up to see a brand-new Bell 429 descending only a few hundred feet away.

The wedding party emerged just as the gleaming new chopper touched down at the end of Main Street. A sign affixed to the passenger door read: JUST MAR-RIED. Trailing was a collection of cans and old shoes attached to the skid rails.

Tom, Claudia, Jordan, and the wedding party made their way up the street as the unseen pilot shut the engine down and emerged from the cabin carrying a leather binder. It was Jimmy Quine, dressed in a very un-pilot-like suit and tie. He approached Tom and they shook hands warmly.

"Sorry I'm late. Hope you haven't cut the cake," Quine said as he handed Tom the binder and gestured at the sparkling new helicopter.

"This is a wedding gift from the governor, President Ayres, and the grateful state of Alaska. Congratulations, Tom."

Seeing Tom's solemn reaction, Claudia intuitively approached him and squeezed his arm. Speaking quietly for fear of ruining the moment for everyone else, Tom said, "It's not right. Being congratulated for killing my own brother."

"You did everything you could to help him," Claudia responded. "And he wasn't your brother anymore. You saved your son, you saved all of us, and, considering that he would have spent the rest of his life either as a guinea pig or a monster, in a way you saved Cooper too. You told Yoshi to move past his guilt—now it's your turn."

Tom remained quiet for a long moment, then finally smiled.

"Like I said—I don't deserve you."

"That's where you're wrong. You deserve me, you deserve Jordan, and you deserve this," Claudia said, gesturing to the adoring crowd looking Tom's way.

As Tom took Claudia in his arms, Jordan approached and said, "Hey, cool sign, Dad."

A puzzled Tom watched as Jordan moved toward the chopper and pulled off the "Just Married" sign to reveal a slick blue and yellow logo and the words BROOKS HELICOPTER SERVICE painted on the side.

Tom turned to Claudia. "You knew about this too, didn't you?"

Claudia and Jordan exchanged glances.

"You're a tough man to shop for."

Tom kissed Claudia and hugged Jordan, then Charlie approached and said with a big grin, "Hey, Tom, better get that thing out of here before I give you a parking ticket."

Tom lifted his bride into the chopper as the crowd started cheering. Then he turned to an expectant Jordan.

"Well, what are you waiting for?"

A jubilant Jordan climbed in the back seat as Tom settled in the front and fired up the chopper. The rotors turned, the engine roared, and the Bell rose to tumultuous cheering from below.

Minutes later, the Bell was angling off to the left above the mountaintops and into the strikingly clear blue sky.

Had Tom angled off to the right, however, he would instead have been flying over the Juneau Icefield where Cooper, his body never recovered, was lost forever. And if Tom had been looking very, very closely, he might have noticed that one large section of ice—and, oddly enough, only this one lone section of ice—was slowly melting where a large ice cave had once been.

THE END

ABOUT THE AUTHORS

Peter Berk has written six novels, three TV pilots, and a dozen screenplays, including several with his father, Howard Berk, which became the basis for the *TimeLock* series of novels. *TimeLock* was a finalist in three cat-egories of the Chanticleer International Book (CIBA) Awards (Science Fiction, Mystery and Suspense, and Global Thriller) and was named a Distinguished Favorite in the TechnoThriller category of the Independent Press Award. *TimeLock 2: The Kyoto Conspiracy* was published in 2023. Peter's political murder mystery, *First Line of Defense,* was released in 2024 and was named a semi-finalist in the CIBA CLUE Awards for Suspense/Thrillers. The same year, continuing the family legacy, his son Jordan's time travel thriller, *The Timestream Verdict*, was long-listed for the CIBA Global Thriller Awards. Peter and his family live in Southern California.

Howard Berk was an award-winning novelist, screenwriter, and producer. His credits include memorable episodes of such classic TV series as *Columbo* (including  "By Dawn's Early Light," which earned an Emmy Award for guest star Patrick McGoohan), *Mission: Impossible,* and *The Rockford Files*, as well as the feature film *Target*, starring Gene Hackman and Matt Dillon.

IngramElliott Publishing

IngramElliott is an award-winning independent publisher with a mission to bring great stories to light in print and on-screen. We publish stories with a unique voice that will translate well into film and television. Visit us at www.ingramelliott.com for more information.

Our IngramElliott imprint features full-length fiction and non-fiction titles designed with the book lover in mind.

Our IE Snaps! imprint features novella-length fiction in popular genres that are designed for a quick read on the go.